Enticing
the Wolf

RAYNA TYLER

ISBN: 978-1-953213-08-2

ALSO BY RAYNA TYLER

Seneca Falls Shifters

Tempting the Wild Wolf
Captivated by the Cougar
Enchanting the Bear
Enticing the Wolf
Teasing the Tiger

Ketaurran Warriors

Jardun's Embrace
Khyron's Claim
Zaedon's Kiss
Rygael's Reward
Logan's Allure

Crescent Canyon Shifters

Engaging His Mate
Impressing His Mate

CHAPTER ONE

REESE

What is he thinking? I stared at the computer screen sitting on the worn and scratched surface of my office desk, then reread the email I'd received from my father. Unfortunately, the message was still the same, and I had four days before Clayton Reynolds arrived and threw my nicely organized life into major chaos.

He'd avoided spending quality time with my sister Berkley and me since we were children, so I had no idea why he suddenly thought a visit was important. Over the last year and a half, I'd spoken on the phone with my father twice, and both times I'd been the one to contact him. The first was to tell him about my grandfather's death; the second was a few days later to tell him he had another son. It irritated me every time I thought about the text I'd received, the one with the lame excuse for not attending his own father's funeral or making time to meet Nick, my recently discovered half brother.

Commitment had never been a word my father understood. He'd been a terrible husband, a worse father, and was never going to win any awards for his parenting skills. He was, however, family, and though I wanted to reply and tell him not to bother coming, I couldn't.

I puffed out a heavy sigh, skimmed my hand through my hair, and glanced at the forest outside my window. Normally, the tranquil greenery had a calming effect, but today it wasn't helping. No matter how much I wished I'd never seen the message or that the damned thing would magically disappear, it didn't alleviate the dread creeping along my spine. A dread that involved upsetting my siblings when I told them about our father's unexpected visit.

Of the two, telling my younger sister was going to be the most difficult. Berkley had grown up resenting our father, especially after he'd abandoned our mother and us to pursue a younger female. Constantly being disappointed by our sire, coupled with a cheating ex-boyfriend, had reinforced her resolve to avoid having a meaningful relationship with any male.

It had gotten so bad that when she'd met Preston, our new head of security, I'd been concerned she'd never accept him as her mate. Fortunately, my longtime friend was a determined cougar whose patience and persistence had eventually gained him my sister's heart.

Nick, on the other hand, was unpredictable. He'd never met our father or asked for an introduction, so I had no idea how he'd react. Berkley and I hadn't known our half brother existed until James Reynolds, our grandfather, had died almost two years ago and left the Seneca Falls Resort to the three of us.

Surprisingly, when I told my father about my half brother, he'd actually admitted to having a brief fling with Nick's deceased mother. He hadn't shared much about the relationship other than to say he'd met Audra Pearson when she worked for a traveling carnival and they'd shared a couple of wild nights together. It was unclear if he'd known she was pregnant before he'd walked away from their brief encounter. Though I knew about his philandering ways, I would have preferred not hearing the descriptive details of how he'd cheated on my mother.

Since he had a habit of shunning responsibility for his children, I wasn't sure I believed him. Though he lacked the desire to tell the truth unless it was beneficial, there was a good chance that Audra really didn't know how to find him after he'd left.

Nick had been a drifter and rarely talked about his life before coming to live with us. If he decided to share any information about his past, it was usually with Berkley. Her persuasive abilities to get people to talk about personal things, even when they didn't want to, was remarkable.

Up until I'd received the email, my father hadn't shown any interest in getting to know his other son. Now he couldn't wait to meet Nick and attend his upcoming wedding. A wedding I was certain he hadn't been invited to. Since my mother had been invited, it wasn't hard to assume he'd found out from one of their mutual friends.

A rap on the door startled me and drew me from my troubled thoughts. My heart rate jumped even higher when Berkley poked her head through the doorway. I'd never heard of wolf shifters having psychic abilities, but my sister had an uncanny way of showing up when I was thinking about her.

"Are you busy?" she asked as she strolled into the room, wearing a navy blue jacket and matching skirt. Even though the lodge wasn't a fancy hotel, it didn't stop her from dressing professionally.

I wasn't ready to discuss our father's visit and hurriedly tapped a few keys to replace his email with a cost analysis spreadsheet. "No, why?"

"Jac is going to be here any minute."

"Who?" Though the name sounded familiar, I struggled to generate a mental image of the person or come up with a reason why knowing him would involve me.

"Jac Dubois…my friend." Berkley flicked her dark

chestnut strands over one shoulder. "I can't believe you forgot."

I was a thirty-two year old dominant male who'd served a tour in the military and traveled to several different countries. Yet one intense glare from those dark-amber eyes had me squirming uncomfortably.

"You know, the photographer I hired to take pictures for our wedding travel packages." She huffed and perched on the edge of my desk.

I rolled my eyes but refrained from letting her know that I'd rather she use the chair sitting on the other side of the small room. The wingback was old, the gray, cushioned material faded and worn, but I didn't have the heart to replace it. It had belonged to our grandfather, and the male had been more of a father to Berkley and me than Clayton ever had.

Between my father's disturbing news and overseeing the construction on the additional cabins we were building, I'd completely forgotten today was the day her friend was due to arrive. Hearing the strain in her voice made me feel worse and reaffirmed my decision to wait to discuss my father's impending visit.

Besides spending the last six months planning Nick and Mandy's wedding, she'd been dealing with her own stress, namely our overbearing mother. Marjorie Reynolds was due to arrive in a couple of days, and Berkley wanted everything to be perfect before she got here.

"You're right. I forgot, and I'm sorry." I leaned back in my chair. "What can I do to help?"

"Hold that thought." Berkley slid off the desk and retrieved a cell phone from her pocket. After studying the screen, she smiled and slipped the device back into her pocket. "I'll be right back, so don't disappear." She hurried out the door, only to return five minutes later.

"Reese, this is Jac," Berkley announced, then stepped to the side to make room for her friend.

I rose from my chair and froze. Either my sister hadn't

given me enough information or I hadn't been paying attention when we'd discussed the hiring details for our new photographer. Any assumptions I'd had about the position being filled by a male were quickly dispelled by the female who walked into my office with a confident, carefree swagger. She had a slim athletic build, and without the help of the half-inch heels on her laced, ankle-high boots, the top of her head wouldn't have reached my shoulder.

The pair of cutoff shorts she wore rode low on her hips, barely hitting the middle of her thighs and exposing a set of shapely and well-muscled legs. Her sleeveless black top clung to ample breasts, and the shirt's short hem gave me a glimpse of tanned skin below her waist. If I wasn't mistaken, she had a tattoo. The inked skin peeked above her waistband near her right hip.

Her hair, which was short and styled in a spiked cut, was an unusual combination of pale golds, browns, and black. I assumed she colored the strands to get such an exotic appearance. Since my wolf's abilities included enhanced scent, I expected to get an unpleasant whiff of the chemicals she'd used. Instead, I was treated to an enticing array of wildflowers, bubblegum bodywash, and the unique aroma of a feline. A feline breed I struggled to recognize. My wolf, curious animal that he was, wanted to take another sniff of her sweet scent, and without realizing it, I'd eased closer.

"Nice to meet you…"

"It's Jac with a 'C,' not a 'K.' Stands for Jacqueline, which I personally find too melodramatic and formal." She shrugged nonchalantly, then continued into the room and stopped near the edge of my desk. "You must be the"— she made quote marks with her fingers—"older brother I've been hearing about. Don't worry, so far everything I've heard has been good." She winked, then held out her hand. "It's nice to finally put a face with the name."

The second our palms connected, a rush of heat passed

between us. A jolt so strong, I felt as if I were holding the end of a live electrical wire. It pulsed through my entire body, one painfully pleasurable wave after the other.

When the sensation subsided and I could finally breathe, could finally think, I glanced from our joined hands to Jac's surprised face. The instant her gaze locked with mine, I knew I was staring into the eyes, a shade of garnet with dark flecks, belonging to my mate.

"No way." She jerked her hand away from me, an adamant denial in her voice.

Apparently confused yet unaware of what had transpired, Berkley frowned, her gaze bouncing from her friend to me. "No way what? Did I miss something?"

As far as recoveries went, Jac's performance was stellar. She turned slightly to keep Berkley from seeing the flush on her cheeks, then swept her hand over the files stacked on my desk. "It's obvious your brother is very busy, so I think we should go." She tugged on Berkley's arm, urging her to leave the room ahead of her. She paused to grip the doorframe before speaking in a tone that held a hint of regret. "It really was nice meeting you."

I wanted her to stay. My wolf wanted her to stay. But I'd been too stunned to move. Judging by the fading footsteps, she'd already reached the other end of the hallway. I'd been tempted to chase after her, the indecision of what I'd say when I caught her the only thing keeping me in place.

All I could do was stare at the empty doorway and wonder why Jac hadn't acknowledged our connection and why she'd seemed determined to keep Berkley from finding out.

The worst part of the whole experience, the part that made my gut clench, was the overwhelming feeling that she was saying goodbye before we even got a chance to know each other.

CHAPTER TWO

JAC

"My mate," I muttered after leaving Berkley in the lobby to handle a problem with a guest. I pushed the glass door leading outside open, not bothering to hide my frustration as I stomped across the parking lot to my car. Of all the males on the planet, why did my friend's brother, Reese, have to be my destined match?

The man was all kinds of yummy with those brown eyes that made me think of a smooth expensive cognac. He had to be at least six feet tall and there was nothing wrong with the way his broad shoulders and firm chest muscles filled out his button-down shirt. If I didn't already know from Berkley that he was ex-military, the short, neatly styled cut of his rich chocolate-colored hair was a definite giveaway.

Once I'd shaken his hand and that sizzle of recognition zipped along every nerve in my body, it took every ounce of my willpower to keep my cat from climbing him like a tree and kneading him with her paws.

Bad, bad, bad kitty. I closed my eyes and dropped my head against the car's frame, hoping the cold metal would help lower the heat still rippling through my body. Trying to push his image from my mind wasn't doing any good either. I'd gotten a whiff of his scent, an enticing combination of musk, sandalwood, and alpha male wolf. A scent that had already imprinted itself permanently in my memory.

Though many of my kind went their whole lives without finding the person who completed their bond, most shifters yearned to find their mates. I knew I should be thrilled that I'd found mine, yet I could think of at least five good reasons why agreeing to accept this particular male was not a good idea.

Heading the top of the list, and what I considered the most compelling, was the secret I'd shamefully concealed since my youth. A secret that I'd done my best to keep from everyone, even my closest friends.

I'd been serious when I teased Reese and said I'd only heard good things about him. Berkley thought the world of her big brother and had always raved about him being a great guy. I tried not to hold his military background against him. At least I had until now.

To say my view of a male who'd served in one of the armed forces was tainted would be an understatement. I'd sworn I'd never get involved with anyone even remotely connected with the military, and it was a promise I had yet to break.

I'd spent my entire youth trying to meet the expectations of an army colonel father. According to him, I'd failed miserably. If he wasn't ranting about one of my many failings, he'd been too busy with his career or dragging my mother and me from one base to another.

Berkley's childhood hadn't been much better than mine, but she'd always had an older brother looking out for her. There were times when I wondered how different my life would have been if my mother hadn't died or I'd had a sibling to lean on.

There were times when I envied my friend. Not only

had she helped her brothers turn the resort into a prosperous business, but she'd created a stable, loving environment for her family, friends, and employees. Something I'd never had.

Though I couldn't ignore the important leadership role Reese played in his family's success, I was doing my best not to find anything redeeming about the male that could possibly make me change my mind about refusing to be his mate.

Boy, did it bite to find out my proclaimed destiny was one of the males I'd spent the majority of my life trying to avoid. Apparently, the great shifter matchmaker, who I truly believed was a female, was having a good laugh at my expense. I wanted to curse the bitch and her vindictive sense of irony.

I stared at the impressive backdrop of ash, spruce, and various other trees, along with the cabins scattered on the distant mountain and wondered what I'd done wrong to earn my current predicament. Not that pondering did any good. Her Shifterness was going to be deeply disappointed because this was another one of those times, and there'd been plenty, when I refused to comply with her plans.

When I'd left Reese's office, my first thought was to get in my car and race back down the mountain without looking back. Berkley and the promise I'd made to take pictures for her brother Nick's wedding was the only thing preventing me from leaving. The event was a few days away, not enough time for her to find a replacement.

I always kept my word, so I had to put my personal self-preservation needs aside and concentrate on the bigger picture. I'd be staying four days, five at the most. The resort stretched across a large amount of real estate in the middle of nowhere on a sparsely populated mountain. Would it really be so hard to avoid Reese for that length of time?

Once the wedding was over, I'd simply tell Berkley that I'd changed my mind, that I didn't want the photographer's job or to make the resort my home. Of course, both those statements weren't true. I'd fallen in love with the place the minute I'd stepped inside the lodge.

I took another deep pine-scented breath to fortify my resolve, then popped the latch on the trunk. I reached inside and pulled out the two large suitcases containing the majority of my wardrobe. After setting them on the ground, I tugged the oversized black bag that looked more like a backpack than it did a camera case out of the trunk and draped the strap over my shoulder. The bag was bulky and awkward, always banging against my hip when I walked. After years of lugging it around, I'd gotten used to it.

I slammed the trunk shut and nearly jumped on the car's roof when I found Berkley leaning against the side with her arms crossed. "Damn it, Berkley. Stop sneaking up on me." For crying out loud, I was part cat and had enhanced senses. So why hadn't I known or at least smelled that she was there? Because my mind was scrambled with thoughts of an incredibly delicious male with kiss-worthy lips, that's why.

Berkley frowned. "How could you not hear me? I was practically scraping my heels through the gravel."

I shrugged. Just because she was stating the obvious didn't mean I had to agree with her. Normally, I wasn't prone to being flighty, but on the rare occasion when I was, I preferred to call it being preoccupied. Whatever. The point was that whenever I was deep in thought, so was my cat, which made it easy for me to miss hearing someone approach or scent their presence.

"Want to tell me what the heck that was all about?" Berkley tipped her head toward the lodge.

"Could you be more specific on the 'that' part of your question?" I swept my fingers through the tips of my short hair, flashing an innocent smile, a technique I'd used during my old man's countless interrogations. Funny how the conditioned response wasn't working on Berkley any more than it had on my father. But hey, it was still worth a try.

"You couldn't get out of Reese's office fast enough." There was an overprotective edge in her voice—typical dominant shifter behavior.

Since the cutesy thing wasn't working, I tried misdirection. "He seemed pretty busy, and you know me, I'm not big on intruding or overstaying my welcome."

"Uh-huh, since when?" She pursed her lips and did the skeptical scrutinizing thing that would make any human cringe.

Lucky for me, I wasn't human, nor did I cower easily, if ever. I crossed my arms, returning her glare with a pleasant smile, intent on waiting her out. After a few tense seconds, she pushed away from the vehicle, then reached for one of my suitcases. I hoped I was wrong, that the wariness teasing my nerve endings, a direct result of her compliant behavior, was unwarranted.

"Come on, I'll show you where you'll be staying," Berkley said.

"Can't wait." I mustered the enthusiasm I didn't feel as I picked up my other suitcase, then followed her back to the lodge's entrance.

"This place has a private area designed for the owner and the employees." She held the door open allowing me to enter first, then directed me toward the same hall we'd used when we'd gone to her brother's office.

I'd hoped to avoid running into him so soon after our first meeting and was thankful when she turned left, then headed down a corridor in the opposite direction.

"You'll be staying in my old room. It's right next to Reese's."

She matched her longer stride to my shorter one and kept pace beside me. She continued to list the lodge's other attributes, but I'd stopped paying close attention as soon as she mentioned that my room was next to her brother's.

"The room has a great view and a patio with easy outdoor access. Later, I'll show you the area we've designated for runs," Berkley said.

There was an unspoken rule about keeping our existence secret from humans, and I assumed the area she was referring to was meant for shifters only.

Berkley turned a corner that led to a shorter hallway with two rooms right next to each other. "Preston and I are on the other end of the main hall. That's Reese's room." She pointed at the wooden door to her left. "He doesn't snore, at least not that I'm aware of, so you shouldn't have any trouble sleeping."

Why did I have to promise? There was no way I'd be able to stay away from him until after the wedding, not if we were practically roommates. A fact my cat was smugly enjoying. Unlike me, the irritating feline couldn't care less about the rules I'd made for myself. She was thrilled with the prospect of being close to her mate.

With a commitment I couldn't get out of, the dread of disappointing Berkley clinging to me tighter than my favorite pair of shorts, and my cat insistently urging me to find Reese, I was back to plotting a way to get even with the divine shifter matchmaker.

"And this is your new home." She smiled, unlocked the door, then handed me the key. Once we were inside, she set the suitcase she'd been carrying near the end of the bed.

"I need to check on a few things in the restaurant. Why don't I give you about a half hour to settle in, then I'll take you down to meet Nick and Mandy."

From the few phone conversations we'd had before I'd arrived, I knew Berkley's role in running the resort had many facets and kept her busy. I was an independent person and didn't require any special attention. Besides, I needed a few minutes to myself so I could figure out how to turn down Reese without making him feel rejected.

"Sounds great." I set my suitcase on the floor next to

the other one, then placed my camera bag on the bed.

"Great, I'll be back soon," Berkley said as she closed the door behind her.

Now that I was alone, taking time to relax and appreciate my new surroundings won out over unpacking. The room had a rustic feel and was quite welcoming. The walls were finished with light oak wooden planks sealed with a clear stain. From the brief glimpses I'd gotten of the lodge's interior, when I wasn't plotting fate's demise, I'd noticed a similar construction throughout the building.

The furniture was made of a darker wood and consisted of a queen-sized bed with a headboard, a small dresser tucked in one corner, and a longer dresser with a mirror. Off to the right on the same wall was the entrance to a decent-sized bathroom. After running my fingertips along the dresser and taking a moment to admire the craftsmanship, I walked over to the wide patio doors and pulled back the blinds.

I was greeted by a brilliant cloudless blue sky, a wall of tall aspens, the ground covered with old pine needles and the occasional cone. The charm and serenity of the view was enchanting, and once again, I was instilled with a sense of belonging, of knowing I could be happy and make a new life here.

As quickly as the feeling swept over me, it was gone, replaced by a gnawing ache and the reality of knowing I wasn't going to be able to stay.

CHAPTER THREE

JAC

As promised, Berkley arrived a half hour later. Instead of heading back into the lodge, she showed me the employees' private kitchen area, then led me outside onto a deck and a path that cut through the trees.

"Why don't Mandy and Nick live in the lodge?" I knew it was none of my business, but curiosity was one of my biggest flaws. It came with being a feline, or so I'd been told. A psychologist would probably say it was the reason I had a rebellious nature and lacked any self-protective responses when it came to engaging in dangerous situations. Not that I was willing to make an appointment to find out.

Personally, I thought I'd perfected the skill as a means to annoy my father. Bradford Dubois, my only living relative, was a harsh man with little tolerance for his daughter. He was, of course, the person who took pleasure in pointing out my failings. The biggest one being that his only child wasn't a male, which he quickly followed up with constant reminders that I had issues with my cat. Issues that made me feel inadequate whenever he brought them to my attention. Issues that bothered him way more than they did me.

"He's part wild wolf." Berkley grinned and ducked beneath a low-hanging branch. She was one of the few people who didn't seem to mind my "speak first, then think about what I'd asked later" way of dealing with life. One of the many reasons we entertained a lasting friendship.

I followed her under the same branch without having to duck. "Wow, that is so cool. Does he get all wolfy without provocation? Is that why he lives out here?" I knew wild wolves existed, but I'd never met one, part or otherwise. They had a reputation for being loners because their animals had a tendency to go feral. "He doesn't have a problem with cats, does he?"

"No, he's…"

I wasn't sure if she was wrinkling her nose because she was thinking how best to answer my question or if I'd touched on a personal topic that was off-limits. "It's okay, you don't need to explain. In case you hadn't noticed, I'm still working on the overly curious thing." Berkley and I had talked about my bad habit on more than one occasion, usually after it had gotten me into trouble and she'd stepped in to help.

"Curious about what?" A guy appeared from behind a tree.

After hissing and scaling the nearest tree, I crouched on a thick branch and stared at the male who'd startled me. He was tall and broadly built, with a killer grin, and scented of wolf. Wolf that leaned toward the wild side if my finely honed cat senses were correct. And they usually were.

"Damn it, Nick." Berkley punched him in the shoulder. "Would it kill you to snap some twigs or something instead of showing up out of nowhere?"

"Wouldn't be any fun if I did that." He laughed and teasingly nudged her with his shoulder.

"Well, if you want the best photographer I know to

take pictures of your wedding, then you'll stop scaring Jac into trees." Berkley's admonishing glare didn't stop the amusement from reaching her lips.

"Apologies, Jac." Nick's grin didn't waver, and he didn't sound sorry. "How can I make it up to you so my sister doesn't leave claw marks on my ass?"

"*Really.*" Berkley snorted and shook her head.

Watching their antics was fun, and I couldn't stop from giggling even if I'd wanted to. There weren't many people who were brave enough to tease Berkley without fear of retribution. I found myself admiring Nick and his ability to handle his sister.

"Apology accepted." I pushed off the branch and landed on my feet next to Nick. Being part feline had its perks, especially when I needed to deal with heights without hurting myself. "I've never seen a wild wolf before and would love to see what yours looks like."

His furrowed brow had me holding up my hand and adding, "No pictures, I promise." Being a photographer who'd traveled extensively, I'd had the opportunity to observe many shifters in their transformed state. Their animals were larger than their natural counterparts, something a human would notice. I took protecting the secrecy of our existence seriously and would never take someone's picture without their permission.

"His wolf is beautiful." A slender woman with honey-blonde hair appeared from between two trees and strolled toward us. She slipped an arm around Nick's waist, and immediately received a kiss on the top of her head.

With his silky black hair and those slate-gray eyes, I'd bet the woman, who I assumed was his mate Mandy, knew what she was talking about. Other than the height and broad-shouldered frame, Nick's appearance was a contrast to his brother's. My mind immediately conjured an image of Reese, his amazing smile, and the way his dark brown eyes had taken on a glowing amber hue during our memorable handshake. I had no doubt Reese's wolf was a spectacular sight, though I didn't plan to be here long enough to see it for myself.

"Jac, in case you hadn't already guessed, this is my brother, Nick, and his mate, Mandy."

"And who's this?" I reached down to scratch behind the ears of the dog who'd arrived with Mandy and was happily sniffing my ankle.

"That's Nick's dog, Bear. We found him living under one of the cabin porches," Mandy said.

"He's adorable." I squatted, then held out my hand so he could sniff it. Instead of performing a cautious inspection, he lunged at my chest with his front paws, knocked me on my rear, then proceeded to lick my face.

"Bear, not cool." Nick pulled his pet off me, his tone far from scolding. "We're still trying to teach him manners." He held out his hand and helped me off the ground.

"I'm really sorry." Mandy pulled a tissue out of her jacket pocket and handed it to me. "He's usually pretty mellow, even with strangers."

I wiped the drool off my face. "Maybe it's a dog-cat thing."

Mandy frowned. "Are you sure? Because he doesn't act like that with Preston."

"Bear knows better than to mess with my mate. He has way bigger claws." Berkley laughed, then tucked her arm through mine. "Come on, I'll show you where we're going to have the ceremony."

CHAPTER FOUR

REESE

I'd been on edge, my wolf growling and pacing, ever since Jac left my office. Now that I'd found my mate, the urge to be with her, to claim her was overwhelming. Some of the tension straining my body eased when Berkley told me Jac would be staying. The news that my sister had given her the room next to mine helped soothe my agitated animal.

The fact that Jac hadn't acknowledged our connection still bothered me. And as much as I wanted answers, I'd never been one to overreact or address a situation without giving it some thought first. I'd remained in my office with the intention of getting some paperwork done and giving her time to get settled. All I could think about was Jac and coming up with the best way to approach the subject of us being mates.

After staring at the same file filled with purchase receipts for over an hour, I'd decided to track her down. Finding the elusive minx hadn't been easy. She was no longer tagging along with Berkley when I found my sister in the restaurant and Nina, our registration clerk, hadn't seen her since she'd arrived.

I was headed out the private entrance to the employee kitchen on my way to see Nick and Mandy, when I found Jac sitting on the railing of the deck. I wasn't sure why she was straddling the wooden beam with her back braced against the side of the building when there were perfectly good, and comfortable, lounging chairs available.

I'd rehearsed what I wanted to say several times in my mind, but the pleasantries I'd planned to start with were overruled by my need for answers. "Jac, we need to talk."

"I'm pretty sure we don't." She lifted her right leg, then slid to her feet before leaning against the railing. "But go ahead, I'm listening."

"You do realize we have a connection, right?" I needed to hear her confirmation, to know I hadn't imagined the heated sensation that had passed between us, that the lingering effects were real.

"Yeah, and?"

What does she mean yeah, and? Being mates was a monumental deal, and that was all she had to say. I stuck my hands in the front pockets of my jeans to keep from clenching them into fists. Didn't she understand how important this was, how important she was—to me? This wasn't like a human's love-at-first-sight notion where the relationship might or might not last. This was special, a rare bond, one that would develop into a deep caring and endure a lifetime.

Most of the shifters I knew dreamed of the day they'd discover the identity of their perfect match. Unfortunately, it wasn't a simple task, and many of them spent their lives searching and never finding their fated mate. At some point, the human side of our natures wanted to settle down, to have a family, to find some form of happiness.

Though my parents fell into the nonmate category and their marriage had ended badly, I hadn't let the experience sway my decision in either direction. Not until recently, when Nick and Berkley found their mates. I'd be lying to myself if I said I didn't envy the bond they shared, and though I wouldn't admit it out loud, I'd secretly longed for the same thing. Now here she was, the answer to my unfulfilled dreams, sounding indifferent and acting as if being together didn't mean anything.

I tried to figure out why she was treating our meeting as an everyday occurrence, a meeting that bored her. Was it because I was a wolf? I quickly dismissed the thought. She wouldn't be friends with Berkley if she had a problem with other animals.

Maybe she was disappointed by my appearance? I'd had plenty of interested females over the years and didn't believe I was a bad-looking guy. She was an adorably petite thing. Though I hadn't scented any fear or noticed her cringe when we met, I wondered if she was intimidated by my height. Or maybe her cat didn't like dominant males.

I could spend all day speculating, but it wasn't getting me any closer to the answers I needed.

Jac must have sensed my dilemma. "Look, I get the whole you-found-me-and-now-you-want-to-make-me-your-mate thing. I really do. But I also believe the great shifter matchmaker in the sky is capable of making mistakes, so I'm going to make this easy for you." She pushed off the railing and stepped closer. "I'm sure you're a great guy, and I want you to know my decision has more to do with me than you."

What decision? This conversation wasn't going the way I'd visualized it in my mind when I'd set off to find her.

"I know you're my mate, but I don't think it's going to work."

Not going to work. How could she make that kind of assessment without getting to know me first? "If you'll just give me…"

She held up her hand and shook her head. "Unlike you, I have a problem with authority, and I'm the opposite of organized. I was a military brat, and my father was, or I should say is, a colonel. I understand the need to be dedicated to your job and how it comes before anything else in your life."

She pressed her palm against my chest, the warmth seeping through my shirt, calling to my wolf and stirring yearnings I'd never felt for another female before. I reached for her hips intent upon pulling her closer. Jac moved fast, so fast that she evaded my grasp and was standing near the sliding glass door.

"I'm also impulsive and like to have fun." She winked, then walked inside, leaving the door open behind her.

"I know how to have fun," I mumbled, not happy with her insinuation or the lack of conviction I heard in my own voice. I followed her as far as the hallway, watching her saunter toward the lobby without a single glance in my direction, adding further injury to my severely wounded ego.

CHAPTER FIVE

REESE

Preston gave the door a single rap, then walked into my office. Besides being the resort's head of security, he was my closest friend and my sister's mate. "Everything okay? I thought you'd already be out inspecting the sites." Preston said, then eased into the chair across from my desk with his usual feline grace, then settled in comfortably by stretching out his legs and crossing them at his ankles.

No, everything isn't okay. "Something came up." I groaned, wishing I'd locked the door for the first time since I'd taken over this office. Any other time, I wouldn't mind the interruption, but today I was preoccupied with Jac and the way she'd nonchalantly dismissed me as her mate.

"By something, do you mean our cute new photographer?" Preston's wide grin produced dimples.

I usually ignored his all-knowing smug attitude, but today it was annoying. If I didn't think my sister would have a problem with me maiming him, I'd punch him for the cute comment.

"I understand she's your mate. Congratulations."

My irritation notched higher, and I gripped the chair's armrests tighter. "How did you find out? Who told you?" I hadn't said anything to anyone. I didn't know anything about Jac, but since she was refusing to accept me, I didn't think she'd tell anyone about our connection.

"Your sister mentioned that it might be possible, but you just confirmed it." Preston straightened his shoulders, proud of his assumption.

Since I couldn't throttle my sister for sharing her observations, I was leaning heavily toward taking my frustration out on my friend.

Preston furrowed his brows. "Am I missing something? Why don't you seem excited about finding your match?"

"I am, it's just…" I leaned forward and rubbed the dull ache building along my forehead. I'd hoped to avoid having this conversation with the members of my family. Since he'd deduced there was a problem between Jac and me, I knew he wouldn't let it go until I'd given him an answer.

He was exceptional at reading people and studied me with his speculative gaze. "Is there something about her you don't like? Is it because she's not a wolf?"

"You know I don't care if she's a feline, though I am curious about what kind." Generally all it took was one whiff of a nearby shifter for me to recognize their animal. With Jac, it had been difficult. I'd determined she was a cat, but there were oddities in her scent that confused me. It kept me from singling out a specific breed.

Preston gave me another one of his annoying grins. Maybe having Berkley angry with me might not be so bad.

"You know, don't you?"

He leaned back in the chair and clasped his hands behind his head. "I have a good idea."

"*And,*" I growled, ready to lunge across the desk and smack the smirk off his face.

"And, you'll have to ask her."

I slumped back in my seat. "I would, except she's made it clear she doesn't want anything to do with me." Being rejected had been bad enough, but saying it out loud made it worse.

"What? Why not?" He dropped his arms, the smile fading from his face as he straightened in his seat.

"Apparently, she doesn't approve of military males. She also thinks I'm a perfectionist workaholic who doesn't know how to enjoy myself."

He glanced around the room. "She might have a point...about the perfectionist part, anyway."

I was proud of the pristine and well-maintained condition in which I kept the office. "Okay, so I like things a certain way. There's nothing wrong with being organized."

"Never said there was." He shrugged, his sympathetic smile not making me feel any better. "You could always ask Mandy and Berkley for some pointers."

"I'm not sure that's a good idea." I was used to doing things myself. I was the one in charge, the person everyone depended on whenever there was a crisis. My self-esteem had already taken a hit. Did I really want to add needing help from my sister and my brother's mate to the list of my shortcomings?

"Why not? If it hadn't been for Mandy, I'd still be trying to convince Berkley to let me claim her," he said.

I might not want to agree, but my friend made a valid point. Mandy and Berkley were close, had been best friends since they were teenagers. She knew my sister better than anyone, including me. That insider knowledge had gone a long way toward helping Preston get past the wall Berkley had constructed around her heart.

In this case, it was Berkley who knew Jac. My sister didn't have the same close relationship she had with Mandy, but she'd been friends with Jac for several years. I only had one mate, one chance at gaining the happiness I watched my siblings enjoy every day. Was I willing to give that up without a fight because of my need to be in control?

My internal analysis of the situation was interrupted by a static crackle from the radio attached to Preston's belt. The noise was closely followed by a deep male voice. "Boss, you there?"

Bryson was a burly bear shifter and a member of the resort's security team. He only checked in when there was a problem to report. My body immediately tensed, bracing for bad news.

Preston frowned and lifted his hip to unclip the radio. "I'm here, what's up?"

"You might want to find Reese and bring him out to the construction site for cabin fifty-two."

"He's right here. We'll be there shortly," Preston replied.

He and I were both aware there was no point in asking Bryson for more information. He was a man of few words who believed visuals were best and didn't waste his time with long explanations.

I was out of my chair and on Preston's heels by the time he reached the door. Dealing with the day-to-day issues involved with running a resort was a normal part of my job. Some of the tasks were tedious and not as enjoyable as others. I preferred having things run smoothly, but in this instance, I welcomed the distraction. It would take my mind off the situation with Jac and keep Preston's inability to stay out of my personal affairs focused elsewhere.

CHAPTER SIX

REESE

All the roads on the resort's property, except those leading to the new construction sites, were smoothly graded and graveled. After a jostling ride in Preston's truck along the rutted surface caused by constant use and a recent storm, we arrived for our meeting with Bryson.

I'd hired West Mountain Construction, a contractor from the nearby city of Hanford, to build three new cabins. They managed all the sites, each in varying degrees of construction. They were also putting the finishing touches on Nick and Mandy's new home and hoped to have it finished the week after the wedding.

A few of the males in the framing crew paused briefly to watch as we got out of the truck, then returned to their work. They knew who I was since I visited the sites daily to ensure they were on track with their assigned deadlines.

Bryson stepped out of a trailer on the opposite side of the site. It was a much smaller version of a mobile home, with metal siding and a window on each of the long rectangular sides. The interior was sparsely furnished with a desk, a couple of chairs, and a slanted table braced against one wall and used to display architectural plans. The trailer was primarily used by the foreman for daily paperwork and to meet with subcontractors.

He headed toward us, his dark eyes filled with concern. I knew by his serious expression that whatever he wanted to show us wasn't going to be good. Most of the time, he was solemn and rarely smiled. At least he used to be until he'd met his mate, Leah. She was the sister of our neighbor Mitch, who was also the local vet. Now, unless there were troubling issues on the job, he was constantly grinning. Hell, every now and then, I was able to engage him in a lengthy conversation. A rarity for the bear who normally didn't have much to say, and when he did, the conversation was short and straight to the point.

Contemplating the reason for Bryson's happiness led to thoughts of my siblings and how finding their mates had changed their lives for the better. It also made me think of Jac, and the tightness in my chest that I'd been ignoring since we'd gotten the call from Bryson returned with the power of a sledgehammer.

From the information Berkley had shared with me about her friend, I knew she held a lot of respect for Jac. The human side of Jac could refuse to accept me as her mate all she wanted, but I'd scented her arousal, knew she was attracted to me. It led me to believe the only thing keeping her from leaving was the commitment she'd made to photograph the wedding.

She might be adamant our mating would be a mistake, but her cat would be drawn to me on a level that would be hard to ignore. I had no doubt that once the wedding was over, she'd turn down the permanent photographer job Berkley offered her, then leave as quickly as possible.

It tore at me to consider the possibility. Was I so set in my ways, so determined to stay in control of my surroundings, that I'd be willing to let her walk out of my life forever without a fight?

Preston tapped my shoulder to get my attention, then

nodded in the direction of the workers. It wasn't hard to grasp his silent communication. Several males in the crew were shifters, which meant they had exceptional hearing. Gossip was gossip no matter who you were dealing with. I preferred not to have whatever issue Bryson had called us about working its way through the local rumor mill.

I gave him an understanding nod, then signaled Bryson to head toward a spot that was far enough away for us to talk without everyone in the general vicinity overhearing us.

Bryson grunted a greeting, then said, "Sorry to pull you both out of the office."

"Not a problem. Why don't you tell us what's going on," Preston said. Since he was in charge of the security team, I generally relied on him to run point until making a decision required my input.

"This way." Bryson glanced at the crew, then motioned for us to follow him. He led us behind the trailer toward an area where several pallets of lumber had been delivered at the end of the previous day.

The metal bands securing the lumber in place had been cut, and a majority of the boards from each stack were missing. From what I glimpsed of the morning's work, there was no way the crew had used that many boards to frame the cabin. "It looks like the boards were stolen sometime during the night."

Having thefts at the resort wasn't something new. I'd dealt with it before when Desmond Bishop, the previous owner of a fancy hotel over in Hanford, had tried to force us to sign the deed to the resort over to him. One of the nonpersuasive methods he utilized at the time was to have a couple of his men vandalize our property. When that hadn't worked, he'd resorted to kidnapping Mandy. My family and I, along with some of my grandfather's friends, had gone after him. Bishop had disappeared during the rescue, and no one had heard from him since.

It happened over a year ago, and because of our

security team and their regular patrols, we hadn't had any similar problems. I hoped this incident wasn't a precursor to his return. "Was anything else taken?"

Bryson frowned and scratched the back of his head. "Not that anyone has reported."

"Who notified you about the theft?" Preston asked.

"That would be Sid." Bryson tipped his head toward the young guy holding up a board and wielding a hammer. "He was the first one here this morning."

Sid was human, in his early twenties, and from what I'd seen, a good worker. "We can talk to him when they take their next break. In the meantime, I need to speak with Shane." Shane Davis was the foreman in charge of running all the construction crews. I wanted to find out if there'd been any issues with the other sites. I also needed to know if more lumber had been ordered and how badly the loss of supplies would impact his expected completion date.

"He's meeting with an inspector at one of the other sites and should be arriving shortly," Bryson said.

"I assume you already checked the area for scents from anyone who doesn't belong here?" I knew from speaking with Shane that he used the same guys on all his crews, both human and shifter. Since Bryson spent quite a bit of his time working this area, he'd be the first one who could tell us if we had any uninvited visitors.

Bryson shook his head, disappointed. "I did and there wasn't anything I didn't recognize."

"Do you think it's possible we're looking at an inside job?" Preston voiced what I'd been thinking.

The contractor and his men weren't the only ones whose scents Bryson would have detected. Several of my employees, males who were part of the security team, would also be included in that list. I hated to think that someone I'd hired, someone I trusted, was responsible for stealing from my family. "It's starting to look that way."

***

JAC

"So, what do you think?" Berkley gazed through the windshield of the truck, her focus on maneuvering around the weathered holes in the road winding between walls of trees.

"It's really beautiful out here," I said, knowing her question referred to the scenery and the parts of the resort she'd already shown me. Silently, my thoughts returned to Reese, and how walking away after I'd told him I couldn't be his mate had been the hardest thing I'd ever done in my life.

I remembered the trek down the corridor afterward and how it had seemed as if I'd walked for miles. I'd heard him step into the hallway, sensed him watching me, and had struggled not to glance over my shoulder, knowing I'd get another glimpse of his pained expression.

I'd spent the last few hours telling myself that this was for the best, that we weren't right for each other, that we'd only end up hurting each other if I accepted our mating. If I was so darned convinced my assessment was right, then why couldn't I shake the nauseously tight feeling in my stomach?

We wouldn't have had the conversation at all if Berkley and I hadn't been in the employees' kitchen when she'd gotten called to the reception desk to handle a guest emergency. After making myself comfortable and munching on two of her home-baked cookies, I decided to wait outside, which was where Reese found me.

Maybe now that we'd had our talk and I'd bruised, more like annihilated, his ego, he'd avoid me for the remainder of my stay. I hated seeing the confusion and disappointment in those beautiful eyes and knowing I was the one who'd caused it. The guilt of what I'd done weighed heavy on my chest, but I hoped in time he'd realize I'd been right about our match.

The road expanded into a clearing, which turned out to be a construction site. She headed for an empty spot between two other trucks, then parked. "I was hoping you wouldn't mind taking some pictures for the resort's website." Her request sounded more like a stated fact and the sweet, coated-with-excess-sugar tone of her voice made my cat's fur bristle.

"No, I don't mind." I glanced at her warily, searching for a smirk, a sneer, or any sign to confirm my steadily growing suspicion that she was up to something.

"Great, because I'd like to add some shots of the construction." Berkley had informed me during our drive that her family was building more cabins. We'd already been to one of the three construction sites. The progress appeared to be the same as this one. I found it strange that she hadn't said something about pictures while we were there. What was so special about this site that she'd waited until we'd arrived to say anything?

After grabbing my camera and following her toward a beat-up metal trailer, I thought I had my answer. Preston had his hand on the open door and was stepping outside. I'd met Berkley's mate earlier, knew he was in charge of security, and wasn't surprised by his presence.

I was, however, shocked to see Reese exiting the trailer right behind him. I faltered and came to a stop. "What is he... I thought Reese was working at the lodge."

"He usually spends most of the day in his office, but he also does a daily inspection of the sites to make sure everything stays on track for completion." Berkley tucked her arm through mine, her grip tight, as if she thought I might try to escape.

She wasn't wrong. I'd already calculated the odds of making it to the truck before her brother saw me. It was too bad I lacked the coward gene or the intelligence to walk away from a situation when I knew it had the potential for trouble. Otherwise, I would have clawed my arm free and made a run for it.

Reluctantly, with a little foot dragging and some silent cursing, I let her lead me toward the two males. Berkley had a devious nature. I'd bet anything she was purposely trying to make sure Reese and I ended up in the same place together.

"Hey, sweetness." Preston pulled Berkley into a hug the second she released me.

"Hey back." She slipped her arms around his neck and gave him a lingering kiss.

My friend had scored a coveted prize when it came to mates. Fate had done a fabulous job on their match. Their personalities complemented each other perfectly. Anyone who spent more than a minute with the couple could see how much they cared about each other.

I glanced in Reese's direction, noticed his scrutinizing gaze, and felt the soul-penetrating intensity of his wolf. I breathed through the heat pulsating through my body and resisted the urge to verbalize my cat's purring.

Thankfully, Preston had relinquished his claim on Berkley's lips. "What brings you two out here?"

Berkley moved to his side so she was facing Reese and me. "I was giving Jac a tour of the resort. She's agreed to take some pictures of the construction progress for the website."

If I thought it would make a difference, I'd point out that I hadn't readily agreed, I'd been manipulated.

"That sounds like a great idea," Preston replied enthusiastically and gave Berkley a conspiratorial wink.

Berkley spoke to Reese. "I know how much you like to show off what you've accomplished, so I thought you'd be willing to give Jac a tour. That is if you're not too busy."

Reese's apprehensive smile turned into a wide-toothed grin. "Not busy at all."

I tugged the strap of my camera bag higher on my

shoulder. Did his eagerness mean he'd misinterpreted Berkley's request, that he believed I'd asked to take the photos so I could spend more time with him? Would he see it as a challenge to initiate pursuit? Seriously, what had I expected? Alphas, especially those who enjoyed being in control, never gave up on anything.

"Great, because I promised Abby I'd help her bake some desserts for the dinner crowd. If you wouldn't mind giving Jac a ride back to the lodge when she's done, I'd really appreciate it," Berkley said.

"Wouldn't mind at all. I promise I'll take good care of her."

I'd been so busy glaring at Berkley that when she nudged me in Reese's direction, I stumbled. I would have landed on the ground if he hadn't reached a hand out to stop me. The brief contact sent shivers across my already heated skin.

"Thanks." I was torn between frustration and the urge to strangle my friend. I couldn't refuse his offer, not unless I wanted to explain our nonmate situation to everyone in the group, along with the handful of workers who pretended they weren't listening to our conversation. Most of all, I wanted to smack Reese for grasping my hand and using the situation to his advantage.

"No problem."

"I guess I'll see you later, then." Berkley turned and walked with Preston back to her truck. After giving him another passionate kiss, she smiled at me and waved, then got into the vehicle and drove off.

A few choice curse words filtered through my mind, along with the urge to grab a handful of my friend's hair and yank it the next time I saw her. Heading into the forest and shifting so I could get back to the lodge before she did was a tempting idea. One I might have considered if I wasn't worried about losing my favorite camera. At least it was the excuse I told myself.

"Where would you like to start?" I slipped my hand

away from Reese, then unzipped my bag.

"Are you talking about taking pictures?" He raised a curious brow, a mischievous glint in his eyes.

"Yes," I hissed, after realizing he was purposely misconstruing what I'd said into a sexual innuendo.

He chuckled. "If you're sure, then we can start over here." He led me to the other side of what would eventually be the completed cabin.

I walked around snapping shots of the workers and the partially framed building from different angles. The surrounding forest provided a colorful backdrop. After snapping twenty or so pictures, I was satisfied I had enough images for Berkley to review.

While I inspected my handiwork in the camera's viewing screen, Reese walked up behind me and hovered over my shoulder. "Those are really good."

"I think Berkley will be pleased." All I had to do was lean back slightly and we'd be touching, an enticing prospect my cat agreed with, but one I struggled to resist. I snapped the cap over the lens, then slipped the camera back into the bag before turning to face him. "Do you suppose you could take me…" Reese was standing closer than I'd expected. Close enough to inhale his alluring scent. Close enough to kiss.

I realized what I'd said sounded like an invitation and quickly added, "To the lodge. I'd like to go back to the lodge." My precocious cat was urging me to include his room in my specifications. Luckily, the arrival of a male I'd never seen before saved me from blurting out my animal's request.

"Hey, Reese, I've got the information on the new lumber you requested." The guy waving a manila envelope as he strolled toward us was tall, with an outdoorsy appearance and scented of wolf. He possessed a cocky grin and walked with a confident stride, a male who was definitely sure of himself. He didn't bother to mask the lustful glint in his dark eyes. A look that said he was used to females hanging all over him and promised wonderful things if I agreed to be alone with him.

Too bad I'd never been one of those females. I didn't swoon and wasn't easily charmed. I had an overbearing alpha for a father who made sure I knew what young male shifters had on their minds. I'd grown up fast, my starry-eyed teenage-girl phase lasting all of a minute.

Most of the guys on base were too afraid of the colonel to ask me out. If not for my independent nature and ability to sneak out of the house like a pro, I never would have seen the inside of a bar or gotten a date.

"Reese, who's your friend?" the male asked, his gaze never leaving mine.

Reese took the envelope he'd been handed, then pressed his palm against my lower back. "Jac, this is Shane Davis. He's the foreman for West Mountain Construction and is in charge of running the sites."

"Nice to meet you," I said, though I was certain I didn't mean it. I couldn't tell if the tension pulsing from Reese's fingertips was because he didn't like the male or if his reaction fell into the protective mate category. A single touch from another male could be problematic and lead to bloodshed. Just in case it was the latter, I refused to shake Shane's extended hand.

"Same here. And if you ever need a job, you can work on my crew anytime." Shane hooked his thumbs in the front pockets of his worn jeans.

I wasn't impressed by his crude attempt at charm or the way his eyes lingered on my midsection, then moved upward and settled on my breasts. The slow perusal made my skin itch, and not in a good way. I'd dealt with guys like him my entire life. Shifters who had more arrogance in their little finger than they had brain cells in their head. Of course, once I let out my cat's claws and demonstrated how well she could flex her paws on their male parts, they made sure never to make the same mistake again.

Before I had a chance to voice my smartassed reply,

Reese grabbed a fist full of Shane's shirt. "Jac's my mate. If you don't want to lose any parts, you'll refrain from making any more insulting comments." Reese released his shirt and gave him a shove. "And keep your wandering eyes to yourself."

Reese was an intimidating force when he was riled, and my stupid cat was getting turned on by his behavior. Okay, so maybe she wasn't the only one who was aroused.

Shane clenched his fists. He didn't seem like the kind of guy who'd back down from a fight, even if the argument was over someone else's mate, so I was surprised when he said, "Sorry, Reese. I was only having some fun, didn't mean anything by it. I didn't scent a male on her, so I thought she was available."

"Well, she's not," Reese growled. If he ground his teeth any tighter, he was going to crack his molars.

Shane had no idea his comment had struck a nerve and reminded Reese that I'd recently spurned him. It was the worst thing he could have said, and if I didn't act quickly, Shane was going to end up injured.

"Damn it, Reese." I grabbed his wrist and tugged. He was big and strong. There was no way I could make him budge, not unless it was his idea to move. Thankfully, he let me drag him away from Shane and the other workers.

By the time we were alone and surrounded by trees, I was furious. I jabbed Reese's chest with my finger. "What part of 'we agreed we weren't going to do the mate thing, talk about the mate thing, or do anything else regarding the mate thing' didn't you understand?"

"I…but he…" Reese scrubbed his hand roughly through his hair, pausing to take a breath. After a few more deep inhales, he showed signs of calming. When he opened his mouth, I was sure he was going to apologize. Instead, he gave me a lopsided grin and said, "I never agreed to anything."

CHAPTER SEVEN

JAC

You'd think with all the moving around I'd done as a kid, relocating from one base to another, that I'd easily adjust to new surroundings. It didn't matter where I traveled, I found it hard to sleep the first couple of nights in a new place. It didn't help that all I could think about was Reese's parting words at the construction site before he'd left me in Preston's care, then disappeared. Or that while I lay in bed punching my pillow because I couldn't sleep, I'd gotten even more frustrated when I heard him enter his room.

It was nearing midnight, I was restless, and my cat had been clawing at me all day to investigate the forest. I tossed aside the blankets and got out of bed, then headed for the patio. I hadn't heard any noises outside my room and assumed that everyone in this part of the lodge was asleep. Shifters had great hearing, and I didn't want to be responsible for ruining someone else's restful slumber, so I quietly eased the door open and slipped outside.

The three-quarter moon I'd seen earlier in the evening was hidden behind a cluster of clouds. Not that I needed the additional natural light; my cat had great vision in the dark. A gentle breeze wafted in my direction, and for a brief moment, I thought I detected Reese's scent.

Realistically, it was impossible because I hadn't heard any noises coming from his side of our shared bedroom wall for the past hour. The logical part of my brain was quick to point out that this was his home and his scent was all over the place. What I was smelling had to be his residual odor.

Even so, I glanced in the direction of his room, noting that the lights were off. Shadows darkened the area beyond the privacy wall separating our decks.

I wasn't going to let my imagination stop me from taking a much needed run and exploring the area without any supervision. I removed my nightgown and panties, leaving them where they fell. With one last glance around the area to make sure I was alone, I hopped off the deck and ran into the forest. Once I was surrounded by trees, I let the transformation wash over me. I heard the familiar snap as bones realigned and fur sprouted all over my body.

It felt good to run, to tear up the ground with my paws. My last photo assignment had lasted two weeks and kept me in a city without any access to a decent, yet private place to allow my animal side some freedom. My cat suffered more from the confining strain than I did, so for the first twenty minutes after transforming, I let her have control to do whatever she wanted. She started by flexing her claws on the trunk of an ash tree, moved on to sniffing the ground, then batted some wildflowers until she caught the scent of a rabbit.

I wasn't sure how long she chased the furry creature through the underbrush. It was more of a playful pursuit than an actual hunt, and ended abruptly when the rabbit found a hole and burrowed deep inside.

By the time I'd worked off my anxiety and the silly feline was done playing, I was exhausted. I knew if I returned to my room, I'd start thinking about Reese again, about how he was on the other side of the wall, and the wicked things I shouldn't be thinking about doing to him if he was in my bed.

I figured spending the night sleeping in the forest was way better than taking my frustration out on my pillow over a situation I'd created. This wasn't the first time I'd opted for a bed made of rough bark. Not all my work centered on weddings and social gatherings. I'd had clients who wanted nature shots, which sometimes required traveling to uninhabited areas. Taking photos of animals in their natural setting required patience and staying downwind. Some of the best pictures I'd taken were from a distance and from treetop level.

I scanned the nearby trees and found one with a nice thick branch about twenty feet off the ground. A quick jump followed by a shimmy later and I was comfortably sprawled and prepared to take a nice snooze. I'd barely shut my eyes when I thought I heard a twig snap. Though some of the forest's smaller animals were nocturnal and didn't pose a threat, it never hurt to stay alert. My cat was a natural predator, and when more twigs snapped, the sound getting closer, I perked an ear to listen.

It wasn't long before the crunching stopped and the intoxicating scent of a male wolf, one I'd recognize anywhere, reached my nostrils.

I opened my eyes and glanced at the ground beneath me. Not only was Reese standing close to the tree looking perplexed, he was carrying my nightgown and underwear.

Unbelievable.

My irritation at being followed far outweighed my cat's desire to rub all over him. When Berkley told me her brother's stubborn streak was worse than hers, I thought she'd been teasing. I should have known the persistent male would have the audacity to ignore my wishes.

Well, destined mate or not, he was about to get a firsthand taste of my kitty's claws.

RAYNA TYLER

***

REESE

I sat on the foot of my bed and tipped my head from side to side, listening for the pop as I stretched the tight muscles. It had been an aggravating and stressful day, and it was late in the evening by the time I reached my room. I couldn't believe how close I'd come to losing control of my wolf. If Jac hadn't dragged me into the forest, things between Shane and me could have ended badly. The need to protect and keep her away from the unmated male had been overwhelming.

I didn't want to give her something else to add to her list of incompatibilities and sent her home with Preston. Once she was gone, Bryson and I had visited the other sites and occupied our time by doing a little investigating. By randomly questioning some of the workers, we'd learned that tools had also been disappearing from all three sites over the last few weeks.

Before making the resort his home, Nick had lived in numerous places, never settling in one place very long. He'd worked for several different construction companies and said it wasn't uncommon to have tools go missing.

Tools was one thing, a large load of expensive lumber being taken was another. Having the two things happen simultaneously might not be a coincidence. So far the cost to replace what was taken was minor, but if it continued, the financial ramifications to the resort could be devastating. I was afraid Preston's theory about someone we knew being the culprit held a lot of merit. It left me with the troubling question of why, and was it someone who wanted to hurt my family.

Contemplating the recent thefts wasn't the real issue twisting my gut into hundreds of tiny knots. It was finding my mate, then being rejected by her without having a say in the matter.

I rose from the bed, grabbed a beer from the mini fridge I'd installed in the corner next to the dresser, then walked outside onto my private deck. This was one of those times when I wanted a break from being in charge and needed solitude without any interruptions. I settled into a cushioned lounger, my thoughts returning to Jac.

I didn't really know the female, yet I couldn't shake the ache from wanting to be near her that I'd been experiencing from the moment we'd touched. My wolf was even worse. His constant growling and pacing was unnerving, and no amount of alcohol was going to dull our overwhelming desire to be with our mate.

I'd finished half the beer and had the bottle raised to my lips to take another swig when I heard the glass door leading from Jac's room to her patio slide open. Shadows hid the chair where I sat. If I didn't move and controlled my breathing, there was a good chance she wouldn't know I was here. I'd expected her to take a seat in one of the chairs or perch on the railing as I'd seen her do earlier. I hadn't expected her to strip, discard her clothes haphazardly, then give me a glimpse of her glorious body. A glimpse that lasted less than a minute but long enough to give me an uncomfortable erection.

She had to be going for a run. It was the only reason I could think of that she'd be heading into the forest naked. She'd dashed into the woods so quickly that I didn't get a chance to see her cat or determine her breed. Not that it mattered, because I was good at tracking. Maybe not as good as Nick, but what I lacked in skill, I made up for in determination. And right now, I was determined to learn everything I could about my mate and had every intention of following her.

I grinned, exhilarated by the thought of a chase. I set my bottle on the railing and walked over to her deck. After gathering her nightgown and black satin panties, which I took a moment to scent, I followed her into the forest.

After five minutes of tracking her cat's erratic trail, it was evident Jac didn't have a particular destination in mind. I made sure to give her plenty of space and stay downwind so she didn't get a whiff of my scent. Trailing after her was amusing and the most relaxed I'd felt all day.

A short time later, her scent got stronger near a copse of massive trees. It was as if she had stopped, then disappeared. I strained to listen, to see if I could detect any sign of movement, but heard nothing.

It hadn't occurred to me that she'd climbed a tree, not until I heard the low warning growl coming from above my head.

"Jac, wait." I barely had time to drop her clothes and hold up my hands before she leaped from the branch. She was twice the size of a domestic cat, with cream-colored fur covered in black spots and dark stripes. Her large paws hit my chest with enough force to knock me backward. I lost my balance, tripped, and landed on the ground on my back.

She shifted during the process, and I ended up with her straddling my waist. I would've been happy to let her sit there as long as she wanted, but while I gasped to replace the air she'd knocked out of my lungs, she rolled to the side and sprang to her feet.

She snatched her nightgown off the ground and tugged it over her head, glaring at me the whole time. "One wisecrack about my cat, or anything else, and I'll leave claw marks in places that will make sitting uncomfortable."

I had no idea what she was talking about unless she was referring to the fact that she was a hybrid. From what I'd seen before she pounced, she was an ocelot, or at least a mixed version of one. Her ears belonged to a larger wild cat, possibly a jaguar, and her fluffy tail definitely belonged to a house cat. It explained why I hadn't been able to determine her breed.

Hybrids were rare. The majority of mated shifter couples produced offspring that took after the father. I wondered if someone had treated her badly, if that was the reason she seemed embarrassed and defensive about her mixed animal. I didn't care if her cat was unusual. I thought she was the most beautiful thing I'd ever seen and would kill to see more of her cat.

I pushed off the ground and dusted the dirt off the back of my pants. "Jac, I…"

"I mean it, Reese. Not one word," she snapped.

Much to my disappointment, she bent over and made sure her ass was covered while she pulled on her panties.

She smoothed out her gown, then glared at me. "Why are you following me?"

Showing up with her clothes made it impossible to tell her I'd simply been out for a walk. I scrambled for a reason and looking out for her safety was the best I could come up with. "Did Berkley tell you what happened to Mandy last year, about the abduction?"

"I vaguely remember her mentioning something about it. Why?"

"It's the reason we have all the security. We wanted to make sure all our employees and guests are safe." I was telling the truth, and so far, my story sounded plausible.

She crossed her arms and scowled. "Are you saying you followed me to make sure nothing happened to me?"

"Yes." I hoped my smile appeared sincere.

"I see."

What does she see? All I'd done was agree with her, so why did I feel like I'd lost control of the situation?

"You're saying you decided to bring me my nightgown, and my underwear, because of the chivalrous notion that I needed to be protected. Not because you saw me leave my room, then lurked in the shadows without saying a word so you could watch me strip."

I cringed because anyone listening to her describe my actions would think I was a stalker. "Exactly."

"Uh-huh." She uncrossed her arms and padded toward me, then stood on her tiptoes and pressed a soft kiss to my jaw. "Thanks for the rescue, but it still doesn't change anything. We aren't going to mate."

I watched her saunter back toward the lodge and willed my wayward cock to relax.

CHAPTER EIGHT

REESE

I sat in my office staring out the window at the blue sky peeking through the treetops and musing about my dilemma with Jac. If she thought she could tell me I didn't have a say in my future, then give me a chaste kiss and expect me to simply let her walk away, she was wrong.

The best way to win a battle was to understand the opponent. It was the most valuable thing I'd learned from my time in the military. I didn't want to conquer or control Jac, but I did want her to change her mind and choose to be with me. In order to prove to her we should be together, I needed an advantage. I needed to learn a lot more about her, which meant I needed to spend more time with her.

Berkley had first mentioned her friendship with Jac when she'd proposed adding the wedding travel packages to the resort's list of accommodations. After seeing the shots Jac had taken at the construction site, I agreed her photographic skills were amazing. Besides being strong-willed and the sexiest female I'd ever seen, with or without clothes, I knew her father was a colonel and that her animal was a uniquely beautiful feline.

After a brief conversation with my sister and a new plan of action formulating in my mind, I pushed away from my desk and headed for Jac's room. I knocked on her door, hoping she didn't slam it in my face.

"Come in, it's unlocked," Jac's voice echoed from a distance.

I walked inside, not sure what to expect.

"I'll be out in a minute," she called from the bathroom.

I moved farther into the room, careful not to trip over the two open suitcases filled with clothes and several pairs of shoes littering the floor. If she hadn't bothered to unpack, was I right about her leaving after the wedding? It was a troubling thought, one I would worry about later. I pushed aside the clothes strewn across the end of the unmade bed and took a seat.

From this vantage point, I could see the back of Jac's partially naked body as she got dressed. She had finished putting on the bikini bottoms for her bathing suit and was hooking the clasp for her top. I also got a better view of her tattoo. It was a jungle cat, the image stretching along her hip, the tail curling along her butt cheek.

It was all I could do to suppress my wolf's growl when she bent over to tug on a pair of cutoff shorts and presented me with an even better view of her ass. I should have looked away, but no amount of willpower was going to keep me from admiring her shapely curves.

The few functioning brain cells I had left, the ones that hadn't been compromised by desirous thoughts, kicked in once she covered the upper half of her body with a T-shirt.

I'd barely lowered my gaze to the floor and clasped my hands to hide the evidence of my arousal when she appeared in the bathroom doorway and froze.

"What the…" She frowned and leaned against the doorframe. "You're not Berkley."

I couldn't resist the taunt. "Nope, but I'm glad you can

tell the difference."

She pursed her lips. "That's not what I meant. What are you doing here, and why are you sitting on my bed?" She grabbed the clothes next to me and tossed them onto the dresser.

"I came here to see if you were ready to go." I got to my feet, determined to take control of the situation before she could find an excuse to kick me out.

"Go where?" she asked.

I ignored her suspicious scowl and flashed her an innocent grin. "To give you a tour of the falls."

She crossed her arms. "What happened to Berkley? I was supposed to be going with her."

"She had to take care of some guest issues and asked me to take you," I said, stretching the truth somewhat. Surprisingly, when I'd asked my sister what the females had planned for the day, she'd been more than happy when I volunteered to be Jac's guide.

"Uh-huh." She warily glanced in my direction as she strolled across the room to the small wooden desk in the corner. "I thought you were busy with all your construction projects. I'm pretty sure I can find the falls by myself." She smirked, picking up a set of keys and a cell phone, then stuffing them in her pockets. "After all, I did manage to travel across several states and find the resort all by my lonesome."

I found her sarcasm amusing and clamped my lips together to keep from laughing. "I'm sure the contractors can survive a few hours without me." I didn't mention I'd already asked Nick and Preston to take over at the sites for me. "Besides, this is your fault."

"My fault," she stammered. "How is this my fault?"

"I decided to take your advice."

"And which one of my worldly words of wisdom did you decide was important? Because clearly you weren't listening when I said you and I were a bad idea."

"The one about making time to have fun. With you."

47

"That wasn't what I meant when I…"

It was the first time I'd seen her get flustered, and the rosy color blossoming on her cheeks was an added bonus. "Coming?" I snatched the bag containing her camera and tugged the strap over my shoulder. I opened the door, pausing long enough to glance over my shoulder and get a glimpse of her stunned expression. "Unless you're too afraid to be alone with me." I tossed out the challenge hoping it would convince her to come with me.

"I'm not afraid of anything." She defiantly jutted out her chin and opened the door. "Especially you."

"If you say so." I closed the door behind me, then watched her stomp down the hallway. The sway of her gorgeous ass was an appealing sight, and I considered finding more ways to make her angry.

***

JAC

Of all the times I'd given a guy advice, why did Reese have to be the first one to actually listen? I shook off my frustration by rushing ahead of him. I told myself the entire way down the hall, through the lodge, and even after I'd planted my ass in the passenger seat of his truck that the only reason I'd gone with him was because he was holding my camera hostage. It had absolutely nothing to do with how badly my cat—not me—longed to sidle up against him and mark his too-sexy-for-his-own-good body with her scent.

Snapping the seat belt into place was a good way to keep the wanton feline under control and put some distance between us. Though it didn't help once Reese was settled inside the cab. His enticing male scent teased my nose and continued to tempt my cat. He hadn't even left the parking lot and I was ready to follow my cat's lead, crawl into his lap, and purr.

As it was, I had to feign a coughing fit to disguise the desirous rumble rising from my chest.

"You okay?" Reese tapped the brake and stopped the truck.

"Fur ball," I said, smacking my chest hard enough to hurt.

"There's bottled water in a backpack behind the seat."

Why did he have to sound so concerned? And why was I appreciating it so much? I cleared my throat again. No amount of water was going to cool the heat coursing through my body. "Thanks, but I'm good."

He let up on the brake, then drove out of the lot, turning left instead of right as I'd expected. "I thought you said we were going to the falls." All the signs I'd seen when I'd driven the long winding road leading to the resort had indicated the popular tourist attraction was in the other direction.

"I know a short cut." He turned left again, putting us on a worn dirt road, the ruts worse than the ones Berkley and I had traveled over the day before.

"I think I would have preferred taking the long way." The truck bounced again, forcing me to grab the edge of my seat and keep a firm grip on the overhead handle near the door with the other. I wanted to ask him if this was his way of torturing me for refusing to be his mate.

Reese seemed unaffected by the jostling and manned the steering wheel like a pro. "Trust me, where we're going will be worth it."

"It better be, otherwise you're paying for my next visit to the chiropractor," I teased. We both knew being a shifter blessed us with enhanced healing abilities. Any aches I incurred today would most likely be gone by tomorrow.

He chuckled, then changed the subject. "How did you meet Berkley?"

"She never told you."

He shook his head. "Nope, but I'm sure there are a lot

of things my sister hasn't bothered to tell me."

I wasn't surprised. The way Berkley and I had met wasn't something you picked up the phone about and immediately shared with your big brother. "We met when she was attending the university."

"You were in the business program too?" Reese shot me a curious glance.

"No, I was on a photo assignment. The school was working on improving their social image and hired me to take shots of some of the buildings, staff, and students." The bumps in the road were less invasive, and I released my grip on the seat. "While I was there, I heard about a bar close to campus that was supposed to be a lot of fun, so I decided to check it out."

"And was it…fun?" he asked.

"Let's just say the atmosphere and drinks were outstanding. It was the guys who didn't like to be told no that caused me problems." I remembered the young males in their early twenties who reminded me a lot of Shane. Arrogant examples of walking testosterone that still needed work on refining their charm.

"Berkley stepped in to help, didn't she?"

I grinned, amazed at how well he knew his sister. "Yep, best bar fight I've ever had. Berkley and I have been friends ever since."

"You've been in more than one fight?"

"A few, but nothing worth mentioning." The few I was referring to involved military males and part of the reason I refused to get involved with them. I was enjoying my time with Reese and didn't want to ruin it by talking about things from my past that might direct the conversation to the topic of us not mating.

He drove the truck into a small grated clearing, then stopped. "There's a secluded area not far from here the tourists don't know about. Feel like going for a hike?"

"Sure, a walk sounds great." It was exactly what my cat needed.

Whether out of habit or the need to maintain control, Reese reached for the handheld radio sitting on the seat between us.

"I thought you said you knew how to have fun?"

"I do. Why?"

I glanced at the radio in his hand. "Prove it," I tossed out nonchalantly. He was a leader, had to be in control. I didn't expect him to accept my challenge. Though I was certain I'd made my point, I refrained from letting my smirk reach my lips.

When he narrowed his eyes, I could almost imagine the internal argument he was having with himself.

"Fine." Reese placed the radio back on the seat and got out of the vehicle.

Just because he'd won this round didn't mean I was going to change my opinion, or my mind, about our nonclaiming situation.

He tilted his seat forward to retrieve the backpack containing the bottles of water he'd mentioned earlier.

I grabbed my camera bag off the floor near my feet, then got out and walked to the front of the truck. "Where to now?" I enjoyed a good hike and was looking forward to the exercise. The area was beautiful, and I planned to take some pictures.

I'd worn my bathing suit under my T-shirt and shorts because Berkley had mentioned there were places near the falls for swimming. With Reese in charge of the outing, I wasn't sure if taking a dip was on the itinerary. I guess I'd have to wait and see.

***

It didn't take us long to reach the area Reese had mentioned. Hidden within a clearing was a pool beneath a wall of boulders forming a small, secluded waterfall. I glanced longingly at the water's translucent surface, contemplating his suggestion to go for a swim, then turned and waggled my finger at him. "Don't you dare remove those pants if you aren't wearing underwear." Being embarrassed by nudity was something I'd grown out of shortly after I'd learned how to shift. If he'd been any other male, keeping his private parts covered while in the water would have been optional. But this was my mate, and the sexual tension between us, the need to be together, the need to claim, sizzled like a live wire stretching between us. Testing the boundaries of my willpower was not something I wanted to do, not with my cat pushing me hard to accept him.

Reese had the button undone and paused with his hand on the zipper. "Afraid of what you might see?"

I jutted my chin. "I told you before, I'm not *afraid* of anything." Intrigued, yes. Afraid no. Actually, I was more than a little curious, but I refused to let him bait me. "I'm serious. No underwear, no going in the water with me."

"I'd let you go in the water naked if you wanted to." He pouted and tugged off his pants, exposing a tight pair of briefs that enhanced an impressive male package.

I hadn't realized I was staring and holding my breath until he chuckled. "Change your mind?" He hooked his thumbs under the waistband. "Because I can..." He pushed the fabric a half inch lower.

I found the strength to jerk my gaze back to his face. "No." I protested louder than I'd meant to.

He shrugged. "Your loss."

Damn, full of himself wolf. His egotistical smirk was enough to remind me that I needed to stick to my plan. There would be no mating, claiming, or anything else happening between him and me. My cat thought differently, but I was doing my best to ignore her snarling arguments.

"You ready?" he asked.

"Go ahead, I'm right behind you." I stepped out of my shorts and reached for the hem of my shirt.

He didn't hesitate to run toward the water's edge and

dive beneath the crystal blue surface. With the falls in the background, the lighting was perfect, and I reached for my camera. I waited for him to resurface, then took several pictures. Where he was standing, the surface of the pool hit his waist. I got some pictures of him swiping the water from his hair, the drops trickling down his gorgeous chest.

"Sorry, I couldn't resist," I said, snapping a few more shots.

Reese didn't seem to mind at all. In fact, he was grinning. I didn't need to see the digital version to know the photos would be droolworthy. I experienced a momentary bout of jealousy when I thought about other females seeing the pictures and panting over him. There was no way the photos would ever leave my private collection.

"If you need more, I could…" Reese said.

I had yet to meet a male shifter who had a problem with his nudity, and he was no exception. He taunted me by slipping his hands beneath the water.

My body heated as an image of Reese posing naked on one of the nearby flat rocks flashed through my mind. Those were the kinds of pictures that fulfilled my photographic fantasies and would definitely keep me awake at night. "I'll keep it in mind."

I set my camera back in the bag. My body was overheating, and I desperately needed to cool off in the water. I hesitated with my hands on the hem of my shirt, not sure if exposing my skimpy bathing suit was a good idea.

He must've guessed what I was thinking. "What happened to not being afraid?"

I'd never been one to walk away from a challenge, and even though I knew I should run from this one, I couldn't. I decided to meet his dare and do a little taunting of my own. I tightened my grip, then slowly inched the fabric upward along my body until I'd removed my shirt. I didn't bother to hold back my satisfied smile when I heard his low rumbling groan.

His appreciative noises emboldened my desire to continue torturing him. I padded toward the water, adding emphasis to the sway of my hips with each step. His gaze glowed amber from his wolf and his mouth was hanging open by the time I reached the pool's edge.

"Still think I'm afraid?" I asked, then dove into the water. What I hadn't counted on was Reese finding a way to get even. I broke the water's surface, opened my eyes, and found myself ensnared in his arms.

"Thanks for the show," he murmured, his voice deeper, half human, half wolf.

I should have backed away, swum to the other side of the pool, anything to put some distance between us. But my cat, danger-seeking creature that she was, wanted to play. And if I was being honest, so did I.

"You're welcome." I pressed my palms against his chest, resisting the urge to knead the firm hard muscles with my fingertips.

It was all the incentive he needed to pull me closer, his thick, hard erection pressing against my belly. Desire filled his gaze. When he lowered his mouth and captured my lips, I surrendered.

CHAPTER NINE

REESE

No female had ever tempted, teased, and annoyed me all at the same time, not the way Jac did. I'd been proud of my restraint, but after her enticing display, I'd lost the ability to think clearly.

Once she was in the water, I wanted her in my arms. When she placed her warm palms against my chest, I lost control. One reserved kiss, encouraged by her soft whimpers, led to another and another, each taste of her lips more aggressive than the last. Before I knew it, I'd possessively conquered her exquisite mouth with my tongue.

Jac's enthusiasm rivaled my own. With a surrendering moan, she slid her hands across my shoulders, her nails digging into my nape, her body seductively rubbing against mine.

I barely had the chance to cup her gorgeous ass and squeeze before the sound of a male coughing filtered slowly through my hazy, desire-filled state of mind. It was the second, much louder and irritating cough that forced me to end the kiss and relinquish the tight hold I had on

Jac.

My wolf snarled, his hair spiking straight along his spine. I released a protective growl before I realized Bryson was standing close to the pool's edge near the spot where Jac and I had recently removed the majority of our clothes.

"What's wrong?"

It took Jac a little longer to react. She glanced in Bryson's direction, her already flushed cheeks growing darker. "Oh," she mumbled, but didn't try to pull away.

"I'm sorry for interrupting, but there's an emergency at the lodge," Bryson said.

He had to be the biggest, most powerful male I'd ever met. Yet he was doing his best to keep his gaze averted and not openly stare at Jac. I had a feeling if I questioned him later, he'd be able to tell me exactly how many medium-sized rocks he was toeing with the tip of his leather boot.

"What kind of emergency?"

"Preston didn't say. He just told me to find you when he couldn't get you on the radio."

Bryson wouldn't have shown up if I hadn't let Jac dare me into leaving the radio in the truck. "Damn it," I muttered, giving her an admonishing glare, then regretting it seconds after I'd done it.

"We should go." She wiggled out of my arms, then waded out of the water. Without saying another word, she donned her shirt and shorts, then grabbed her camera bag and headed for the path leading back to my truck.

I almost felt sorry for Bryson. Unless Berkley or Preston had said something, he had no way of knowing Jac was my mate, or that I'd be pissed at anyone who interrupted us. He didn't say anything, but he was an intelligent male, and by the way I'd reacted, he had to know.

I groaned and headed out of the water. "How did you find me?"

"Used the GPS on your truck."

I was glad the safety measure we'd implemented worked. But short of someone dying, there wasn't an excuse good enough to appease my irritation.

Bryson waited patiently for me to pull on my pants. "Sorry about Jac. If there's anything I can do…"

I wasn't in the mood to explain the intricacies of my nonrelationship with Jac or how I'd just made it worse. "Not your fault. I messed up, and I need to fix it." I grabbed my shirt and trailed after my mate.

***

Growing up with two females, I'd learned it was better to wait for their anger to cool to a slow simmer before trying to engage them in conversation. Apparently, Jac was no different. She spent most of the return trip staring out the window without speaking to me. Not that I blamed her. With one stupid comment and a flash of my temper, I'd given her the justification she needed to support her claim against us mating.

It didn't matter how right she'd felt in my arms or how much my wolf and I craved her touch. The damage was done, and if I didn't find a way to repair it, she was going to leave.

The closer we got to the lodge, the more I realized I hadn't been upset about relinquishing control as much as I was about having my time with Jac shortened. When I got her alone again, and I was determined it would be soon, I'd find a way to tell her. Though showing her would be better, I had no idea how I was going to make it happen.

As soon as we reached the lodge and I'd parked the truck, Jac had her belt unsnapped and was grabbing her camera bag. "Thanks for taking me to the falls." Her voice lacked enthusiasm, and I was sure she didn't mean it. "I guess I'll see you later." The truck door had closed and she was almost to the lobby's entrance before I had a chance to say anything.

Great. Any headway I'd hoped to gain during the trip to the falls had ended in failure. I'd always worked hard to be successful, because failing, and the gut-wrenching emotions that accompanied it, was not something I enjoyed. Weighted down by my own self-inflicted disappointment, I slammed the door and stomped toward the lobby.

I needed to put aside my personal problems and find the strength to deal with whatever emergency Preston thought warranted sending Bryson to find me. I was halfway to the reservation desk when Nina glanced away from the guest she was assisting to speak to me. "They're waiting for you in your office." She cringed and bit the corner of her lip.

They? Dread settled in my chest. Whatever was going on had to be bad for Nina to sound so concerned. Normally, I liked to be prepared when it came to dealing with any crisis situation. I would've asked Nina for more details if we'd been alone. But with a paying customer listening to our conversation, I'd have to find out what was going on in my office without getting any further details.

When I reached the hallway that led to the employee area of the lodge, I considered going to my room first to change out of my damp clothes. The decision to postpone dealing with whatever drama was going on in my office changed when I heard Berkley's raised voice. "You can't be here."

"I have every right to be here. He's my son." My father's bellow breached the gap of the partially opened door and echoed through the corridor.

"Yeah, a son you've neglected to acknowledge until now."

I pushed the door open the remainder of the way, then paused in the entryway. Berkley was hovering over my desk, her hands pressed firmly on the surface. My father was seated in the visitor's chair, scowling, his hands tightly clenching the armrests, and I expected to hear fabric shredding any second.

Preston had taken a position in the middle of the room and was leaning against a filing cabinet, ready to step between them if things turned ugly. Or uglier than they already were. He glanced in my direction, his tense gaze begging for assistance.

"Reese didn't seem to have a problem when I told him I'd be arriving for the wedding," my father said.

Fuck. "Wait, that's not..." I remained in the doorway in case my sister decided to throw something. Shifters were stronger than humans. Berkley had a temper, rarely missed, and there were several sharp objects sitting on my desk. Things like the letter opener, the stapler, and the picture of my siblings that I'd taken shortly after we'd moved into the lodge.

"You what?" Her scathing glare made me wince. "Why didn't you talk to Nick and me first before you told him it was okay?"

"Berkley, I'm sorry and you're right. I should have told you." But Jac had arrived, and I'd been so focused on her that I'd completely forgotten about everything else. Besides, my father wasn't supposed to arrive for a few more days.

"And just so we're clear." I turned to my father. "I never agreed to your visit, but now that you're here, I want to know why."

***

I possessed more patience than Berkley when it came to dealing with our father. I waited for Preston to do as I'd asked and escort my sister from the room before closing the door and circling behind my desk. "Let's have it." I motioned for my father to return to his seat, then slipped into my chair, the old leather squeaking under my weight.

"Have what?" my father asked as he settled back into

his seat.

His reluctance and avoidance when addressing an issue were techniques I was quite familiar with. "The real reason you finally decided to visit us." I crossed my arms and glared, unwilling to give him any leeway.

"Like I said in my email, I wanted to meet Nick and show my support for his wedding."

"You've known about Nick for over a year and haven't shown any interest in meeting him. So why now?"

"I was nervous about his reaction," he said.

He appeared calm, but something about his explanation sounded off, and I wasn't buying it. My father never did anything that didn't benefit him, including using his children for his own personal gain. Arriving earlier than he'd stated in his email boosted my level of wariness.

"And…?" I leaned back in my chair, unwilling to end our conversation until I'd discovered what prompted his visit.

"I know I've made a lot of mistakes with Berkley and you. Mistakes I'll never be able to fix but would like to try if you'll let me." He scrubbed his hand through his hair, the dark strands streaked with more silver than the last time I'd seen him. I noticed a weariness I'd never seen on his face before. Even his chestnut eyes lacked their usual intensity.

The speech, however, was something I'd heard him say to my mother numerous times. Usually after she'd found out he'd been cheating on her. It was also the same thing he'd said in a slightly different version shortly before he'd walked out of our lives. Arguing or reminding him about his past behavior wasn't going to help the current situation. "You're going to have to do better than that if you want to stay."

His gaze drifted to the view outside the window before returning to me. "Katie kicked me out."

My father was the one who left females, not the other way around. Katie was his latest conquest. I'd spoken on the phone with her only once, when I was trying to reach him. She'd sounded intelligent, and I often wondered what she was doing with him.

"She told me she was tired of my bullshit, and if I wanted to have a life with her, I needed to make amends with my family," he said.

Definitely intelligent. "Why not find another female?" Even though some of the old resentment about the way he'd tossed his family aside rose to the surface, I kept the sarcasm out of my voice. "We both know commitment isn't your thing."

He slumped his shoulders, the lines around his eyes prominent with worry. "Because Katie is my mate and won't let me claim her unless..." His voice deepened with distress.

I hated to think my father and I had something in common, but I understood the pain associated with a mate's rejection. I wasn't interested in sharing my personal problems or comparing notes, so I moved on to the next hurdle he'd have to address if I allowed him to stay. "You know Mom is going to be here, right?"

"I assumed as much." He was back to masking his emotions. Either he didn't care, which wouldn't surprise me, or he didn't want me to know the information bothered him. "How's she doing?"

A lot better now that you're not in her life. "Fine. She's doing fine." And she was. I hadn't lied.

"Glad to hear it. I look forward to catching up."

If my mother got upset about him being here, I didn't think he'd like her idea of catching up. Possibilities were strong that their conversation might involve his male parts and some bloodletting.

If their interaction reached that point, I was certain Berkley would get involved, more to help my mother than my father. If I knew my sister, she'd called my mother the minute she'd left the room, no doubt encouraging her to sharpen her claws.

I massaged my nape. Thinking about what could happen when my parents ended up in the same room together only made the knotted muscles in my neck tighter. I believed in giving people another chance even when they didn't deserve it. As much as I wanted to appease Berkley, I couldn't bring myself to ask my father to leave. Not after what he'd shared with me and not without a good reason. "I'll allow you to stay on two conditions."

Relief shown in his gaze, and the tight muscle in his jaw slackened. "Name it."

"One, Nick has to be comfortable with you being here." My brother and I might not have grown up together, but it didn't stop me from caring about him or respecting his wishes. I would never force him to accept a father he'd never met.

"And the other?" My father was never one to agree to ultimatums, yet he appeared more than willing to agree to whatever I asked of him.

Had finding Katie changed him, forced him to be a better man? "You need to have this same conversation with Berkley and work things out with her."

"Your sister is pretty angry with me. What if she doesn't want to listen?" my father asked.

"Then find a way to reach her." They'd been at odds for way too long and might never have a good relationship. It didn't mean they couldn't be civil to each other.

"All I can do is promise I'll try."

"That's all I ask," I said.

Filled with apprehension, I silently braced for the upcoming conversation I was about to have with Berkley and Nick. I pushed out of my seat and grabbed the suitcase sitting near the door. "Good, then let's go find you a room."

"Thanks, son." He stood and clamped a hand on my shoulder. "You won't regret this."

I hoped he was right. Because father or not, if he caused anyone I cared about any pain I'd toss his ass down the mountain myself.

CHAPTER TEN

JAC

Reese hadn't said anything on the return drive to the lodge, but the tension filling the cab was unmistakable. I couldn't tell if he was upset we'd been interrupted or because I'd dared him to leave the radio behind. The accusatory glare he'd given me after Bryson arrived assured me that he blamed me for missing the call.

I'd let down my guard and questioned my decision to avoid becoming his mate. I'd teased him and let him kiss me—more than once. Kisses so masterful and hot that my lips still tingled.

Worse, I'd kissed him back, gotten so aroused I'd been seconds away from climbing all over his body, and would have if Bryson hadn't interrupted us. I should've known better, shouldn't have broken my own rules. We were too different. Reese's constant need for control would only lead to heartache, namely mine.

I'd taken his silence during the trip back as a sign that he'd come to the same conclusion. I wanted to make things easy for both of us. As soon as he stopped the truck, I gave him a quick thanks and hurried inside the lodge.

Nina was helping a guest so I waved, then headed for the door reserved for employee access only. I hadn't gotten far before hearing Berkley's raised voice. She was arguing with a male, which I assumed was the source of the emergency. I'd had enough family drama growing up and didn't want to be caught in the middle of theirs. I avoided the hallway that led past the offices and took the one leading to my room.

After hearing Berkley call the male "Father," it didn't take a genius to figure out that her sire had shown up unexpectedly. The fact that my friend had a good set of lungs when she was angry, and I'd heard a portion of their argument, confirmed my suspicion.

When she arrived in my room a little later, rippling with agitation, I didn't ask about the outcome. It wasn't any of my business. If at some point in the future she wanted to discuss the strained relationship with her father, I'd be more than happy to listen. I appreciated my friend's perceptive talents and was glad she didn't question me about my outing with Reese.

She'd stopped by to invite me to an informal dinner with her family and members of the small wedding party. My first impulse was to refuse. I was an expert at avoiding tense family-related situations. Judging by the argument I'd overheard, things couldn't get much more tense. She didn't need to tell me the upcoming meal was going to be difficult for her.

Berkley had been there for me, a shoulder to cry on when things got tough with my father. I figured the least I could do was show up and return the favor by offering my support. Even if it meant I'd be spending time with Reese.

My cat, who'd been annoyed with me for walking away from him earlier, purred at the prospect. She wasn't happy about being away from her mate. I refused to admit I wasn't happy about it either. Not after we'd shared those memorably delicious kisses at the falls. Kisses that left me aching and wanting more.

My rational, less emotional side, the one that understood hurt and rejection, wasn't willing to risk my heart and my future. I wasn't going to give in to Reese even if he could make my body overheat like a flipping volcano. Thinking about our next interaction was the reason I'd dawdled and taken my time showering and changing.

Though wearing cut-offs and a T-shirt was more my style, they weren't the most appropriate clothes for an evening event. After digging through my suitcases, I found a slim-fitting sundress and sandals. I told myself the extra time I'd spent fussing over my hair and finding the right outfit was to make a good impression on my friend's family and had nothing to do with the prospect of seeing Reese.

I rarely had trouble being punctual, but if Berkley questioned my tardiness, I planned to use Nick as my excuse. Meeting his father for the first time was all about family. They didn't need an outsider witnessing the event, especially if the outcome was unpleasant. And by unpleasant, I'd been thinking about Nick and the possibility of his wolf going feral. I still wanted to see his animal, but preferred it to be from a distance and not in the lodge's dining room.

I also figured if anything went wrong, Berkley and Reese would know how to handle it better than me. My cat could move fast, but their animals were bigger and stronger, more equipped to handle an angry wolf.

I pushed aside my worries when I reached the lobby and saw that the restaurant was busy. Berkley said they'd be using a room reserved for private parties. After checking with the hostess to find out where I was going, I made my way to the back of the dining room.

From the outer hallway, I got a glimpse of the left half of the room. There were a handful of people standing in small groups and engaged in conversations. Mandy was smiling and chatting with an older couple who appeared to be in their late fifties.

Bryson had changed out of his uniform into a button-down shirt and pants. He had his arm wrapped around a female with light brown hair. The top of her head barely reached his broad shoulders. I assumed she was his mate, Leah. The male standing opposite them, the one who was laughing and getting his arm smacked by the female, had to be her brother, Mitch. According to Berkley, he was the local vet and a close friend of their family.

Everyone appeared to be enjoying themselves, but I sensed an undercurrent of tension. I got concerned when I didn't see Berkley or Nick, then realized if there'd been a problem, Mandy wouldn't be far from her mate. I slowly inched through the doorway. I couldn't stop myself from scanning the rest of the room searching for Reese, then being disappointed when I didn't see him.

Since Mandy's group was the closest, I headed in their direction. Maybe I'd be able to find out how the meeting had gone. I hadn't made it far when a male stepped in front of me, and asked, "Are you a friend of the bride or the groom?"

Though his hair was several shades darker and streaked with silver, his height and features were similar to Reese's. I didn't need an introduction to know the male was his father, Clayton Reynolds. The whiff of whiskey I scented on his breath came from the half-drained glass in his hand. His charming demeanor seemed forced, his gaze anxious and unsettled. He was a man who was troubled and doing his best to conceal it. Maybe the talk with his youngest son hadn't gone well after all.

"Neither…" I managed to say before Mandy was at my side. "Mr. Reynolds." She ground out his name as if it were a bad word. "This is Jac. She's the photographer who will be taking the pictures for our wedding."

"Nice to meet you, Jac. You can call me Clayton, or Clay, whichever you prefer." He swallowed the last of his drink. "I'm the father, the unwanted interloper." The humorous comment conflicting with his forced smile.

"You wouldn't mind if I steal Jac to help Berkley and me in the kitchen, would you?" Mandy took my hand and pulled me away from Clayton before he had a chance to answer.

She waited until we were out of earshot, even by shifter standards, before letting go of my hand, then said, "I know he's Nick's father, but I don't like him. I've known Berkley a long time, and he was the worst father ever. Is it wrong that I'm not thrilled about him being here, or that I don't think he deserves a chance to be a part of my mate's life?"

"There's nothing wrong with being protective of the people you care about." The direction of Mandy's relationship with her soon-to-be father-in-law was something she needed to decide on her own. I believed people should be given a second chance, but I also knew what it was like to have daddy issues. I didn't want to influence her decision by voicing any negative opinions.

She tapped her chin and absently stared at the floor. "You're right." She snapped her head in my direction, then resumed walking. "As long as he's making an effort to fix things, I should give him a chance."

I found it amusing that she caught what I'd been thinking without me having to say it. If Clayton was sincere about wanting to improve the relationship with his children, then Mandy would provide a good buffer to make it happen. I was more concerned about Berkley and how she was dealing with things.

We'd barely reached the hallway leading to the employees' kitchen when the tantalizing aroma of lasagna filled the air. My friend's cooking was legendary, and my mouth was watering by the time we entered the room. I pressed my hand against my stomach, hoping to suppress the rumble.

Berkley was standing in front of an open oven. There was an apron tied around the back of her waist, and she was lifting a large glass pan off a rack with protective mitts. "Hey, Jac. I'm so glad you came." She placed the pan on top of the stove.

"Wouldn't miss it," I said.

Her quirked brow reminded me of Reese. "Uh-huh."

"Everything okay with Nick?" I wanted to ask about Reese too but didn't want to encourage any more of Berkley's interference.

"Things didn't go well when he met his father, so Reese took him outside to get some air." Mandy picked up a fork and absently smacked the counter with it. "You know, to keep him from doing the wolfy thing."

I nodded, glad Nick hadn't lost it and happy, even though I shouldn't be, that Reese would be making an appearance later.

"Can I help with anything?" I offered out of politeness. My father had done his best to teach me all the things a son should know, things that didn't involve a kitchen. The few culinary skills I'd learned from my mother before she'd passed away included being proficient at reading the instructions on the back of a box and operating a microwave.

"There's a salad and some dressings in that large refrigerator behind you. If you wouldn't mind taking them out to the table, that would be great." Berkley finished cutting the lasagna into serving portions, then put on her mitts and carried the pan out of the room.

Mandy pulled open the refrigerator door. "I'll grab the dressings if you want to get the salad."

"Deal," I said, relieved I wouldn't have to assist with anything complicated. I reached for the large plastic bowl filled with lettuce, chopped tomatoes, olives, and chunks of cheese.

By the time Mandy and I returned to the meeting room, everyone except Berkley had taken a seat. Besides the empty spots next to Nick and Preston, which I assumed were for their mates, the only other seat available was the chair next to Reese. How was I supposed to sit next to him through an entire meal and pretend I wasn't affected by his presence?

Escaping wasn't an option, not with Berkley closing the door as soon as I walked into the room. With all the grace I could muster, I placed the salad on the table, then walked around the table and took a seat. The second my backside connected with the cushion, Reese draped his arm over the back of my chair. He leaned close, sniffed my neck, then whispered, "You look beautiful."

The compliment was unexpected and so was the heat rising on my cheeks. Normally, when a male made comments about my looks, it didn't faze me much. Was that his way of apologizing or another attempt to get me to change my mind?

I turned my head and met his gaze. My lips were inches from his, and the memory of our kiss swirled through my mind. Taking a deep breath and gathering what little resolve I had left, I whispered back, "Thanks, but whatever you're planning isn't going to work."

He raised a questioning brow, then grinned innocently. "Who said I was planning anything?"

***

REESE

Once Nick got over his initial shock of meeting our father for the first time, things hadn't gone nearly as bad as I'd imagined. He might not have liked some of my father's answers and been a little angry at first, but at least he hadn't gone feral. The walk we'd taken before returning to the private dining room for dinner had also helped.

I'd wanted to apologize to Jac for my behavior at the falls. After seeing her in the revealing sundress, then getting a whiff of her bubblegum bodywash, all I could manage was a compliment. Instead of anger, she'd responded with playful banter, which sounded a lot like a dare.

Berkley's decision to serve lasagna had been a wise choice. Conversation remained light and centered on the upcoming wedding. The tension circulating around the room had lessened considerably during the meal.

By the time we'd finished dessert and the additional guests had left for the night, my family had settled into pleasant conversation.

"The lodge looks great," my father said, reaching for his glass of water. "It's been a long time since I've been here, and I'm impressed with the changes you've made. Looks like you three are doing pretty well for yourselves."

Something about my father's comment made me tense, but I wasn't sure why. Berkley and I had been shocked when we'd discovered that the resort had been left to us and Nick. That our father hadn't inherited anything. He'd never said anything about it, and I still wondered if Katie was the real reason he was here or if it was a ploy. A way for him to gain what he thought should have been his. I wanted to believe him when he'd said he was here to make amends, that he didn't have another motive. A motive that benefited him and would upset my siblings and me.

Berkley must have had a similar reaction. Before anyone else got a glimpse of the claws sprouting from her fingertips, Preston had pulled her hand under the table.

"I'll take you on a tour tomorrow and show you the rest of the renovations." Maybe some alone time with my father would provide me with the answers I needed. It would also keep him away from the lodge when my mother was due to arrive.

"I'd like that." He pushed his chair away from the table. "Berkley, the meal was wonderful, but if you don't mind I'm going to head back to my room and call Katie."

"Not a problem." Her gaze softened with a hint of a smile. "We'll see you in the morning."

Now that the meal was over and the group consisted of

my siblings and their mates, I leaned back in my seat and relaxed by draping my arm across the back of Jac's chair.

I glanced at Berkley, then Nick. "I already told him if he does anything anyone doesn't like, he's out of here." Because of the loner lifestyle Nick had lived before we met him, it had taken some time for him to adjust to having a family. The last thing he needed was for our father to ruin his wedding.

"Thank you," Berkley said, then leaned against Preston with her head on his shoulder.

The day had been hectic, and I hadn't gotten a chance to talk to Berkley and Nick about the thefts on the construction sites. I hadn't wanted to discuss the topic in front of our father and was glad he'd decided to retire early.

I didn't have a problem with talking about family business in front of Jac. She was my mate, whether she wanted to be or not. When she acted as if she might leave, I placed my other hand on her thigh, urging her to stay.

"Preston mentioned you were having some problems out on the sites. Care to fill us in?" Berkley asked.

I spent the next few minutes telling them about the disappearing tools and missing lumber. During the explanation, I swept my hand across Jac's bare shoulder and ended up playing with the strap of her dress. When I ignored her shrugs and refused to move my hand, the devious feline purposely scooped some icing off her plate, then slowly licked it off her finger.

I was highly aroused, bordering on frustrated, and refused to let her out-taunt me. I skimmed the side of her neck and gently tugged her earlobe. She squirmed and bit her lip. As soon as I returned to playing with her strap, she slipped her hand underneath the tablecloth and placed it on my thigh.

One slow inch at a time, she slid her hand along the inside of my leg until she brushed against my crotch.

"Jac," I cautioned.

"Hmm?" she said innocently, then dug the tip of her claws into my leg. Not hard enough to cut through fabric, but sharp enough to let me know she meant business.

In my haste to extract her nails, I knocked over my glass of water. It spilled on the table and splashed the front of my shirt, the cold water seeping through to my chest.

"You okay?" Mandy, who was sitting on my other side, giggled and handed me a napkin.

"Fine," I growled and dabbed the wet spot on my chest. If anyone had noticed what had transpired between Jac and me, they were pretending they hadn't seen anything.

Mandy shifted in her seat so she was leaning up against Nick. "Why would anyone want to steal from a construction site?"

"Most likely for the money." Nick curved his arm around Mandy's waist. "It's not uncommon for workers to steal small items, report them missing, then turn around and sell them for a profit. I came across it a couple of times when I was working construction. I don't recall anyone ever having a problem with supplies going missing. At least not in the quantities reported."

"If supplies continue to disappear and we have to keep waiting for new deliveries, the delays will also impact our cost and we'll start losing money."

"What are we going to do?" Berkley asked.

"I've got Bryson increasing security and having the team do frequent checks throughout the night," Preston said.

"Do you think it's an inside job?" Jac turned to address the group.

"We're considering the possibility." Trying to figure out the reason behind the thefts was frustrating. The thought of someone purposely trying to hurt our business was troubling.

"Do all the sites run temporary lighting at night?" Jac's contemplative smile, combined with the way she tapped the table, made me nervous.

"Yes." Instinctively, I knew I wasn't going to like whatever she was thinking.

"I have long-range capabilities with my camera. I could do an overnight stakeout. If the thieves show up again, I can take photos without them knowing I'm there." Jac ignored me and glanced between Berkley and Nick. "What do you think?"

"I think it's a great idea," Berkley said.

Nick shrugged. "Couldn't hurt."

"Absolutely not. It could be dangerous. I won't have my..." I clamped my mouth shut before I said the word "mate."

Jac patted my cheek and got up to leave. "It's so cute you assumed I was asking for your permission, or that you think you can order me around."

CHAPTER ELEVEN

JAC

I hadn't gotten much rest the night before, not because I was still getting used to sleeping in a new bed, but because I couldn't stop thinking about Reese. It didn't matter that my human side had chosen to refuse our mating; my animal side refused to listen. Once a shifter discovered the identity of their mate, their primal animalistic nature took over. The longer I was around Reese, the harder it was to fight the urge to claim him. Knowing he was in the room right next to me, and remembering how hot he'd looked in the pool at the falls, sent my mind into a flurry of fantasies that kept me from getting much sleep.

Berkley was the reason I'd been sitting on the sofa near the fireplace in the area opposite the lobby for almost an hour, drinking my third cup of coffee and enjoying the warmth filling the room from the midafternoon sun. She'd sent me a text letting me know she'd be arriving shortly after picking up her mother from the airport, and asked me to meet them.

I stared out the large bay window at the panoramic

view of the resort's property. The leaves covering some of the trees varied in multiple shades of green and provided a colorful setting to the glimpses I got of the cabins.

I'd been trying to relax, to keep my mind from straying to thoughts of Reese…again. The male had a lot of nerve. He'd assumed the role of attentive mate without apologizing for being a jerk at the falls first. All through dinner, he'd teased my nape with his fingertips, brushed the skin on my shoulder, and played with the strap on my dress. I smiled smugly, remembering his reaction when I'd placed my hand on his thigh, and then inched close to his crotch, and how easily my touch had aroused him. Most of all, I enjoyed letting him know I had claws and wasn't afraid to use them.

I'd heard Reese leave his room early this morning and assumed he was working, possibly visiting the construction sites and giving his father a tour. He was most likely doing his best to keep his sister happy by occupying his father and keeping him away from the lodge during their mother's arrival.

The door to the lobby swung open, and Berkley entered dragging a rolling suitcase by the handle. Marjorie Reynolds walked behind her carrying a smaller case with a matching blue suede finish. She was a few inches shorter than Berkley, but had the same dark hair intermingled with several different shades of brown. Her eyes were a deeper shade of amber and matched her silk blouse.

"Jac," Marjorie waved, her sweet voice carrying across the room.

"Hi, Marjorie," I said, setting my cup on the wooden rectangular coffee table in front of me, then getting to my feet.

"I thought we agreed during your last visit that you were going to call me Mom." She set her suitcase on the floor, then pulled me into a firm hug.

I didn't remember agreeing to comply with Marjorie's insistent wishes, and I knew arguing wouldn't do me any good. The last time I'd seen her was over Thanksgiving weekend a few years ago. After my mother died, my father refused to celebrate, and I usually ended up alone on the holidays. When Berkley found out I didn't have any plans, she used her persuasive skills—more like strong-armed me—to convince me to go home with her. Reese had been stationed overseas and unable to visit; otherwise, we would have met a lot sooner. "It's so good to see you."

"I heard the good news." Marjorie excitedly clasped her hands together.

"What news?" I panicked for a moment, wondering if she'd found out I was her son's mate. Marjorie was relentless. There was no way she wouldn't interfere. She wouldn't leave the resort until she'd done her best to make sure I'd accept him. I wouldn't put it past her to sit outside the bedroom door to make sure we'd completed the claiming.

"Berkley told me you'd be taking the pictures for the wedding."

I released the breath I'd been holding. "Oh, yes, of course."

"Mom, why don't you let me show you to your room, give you some time to unpack," Berkley said.

"I can unpack later," Marjorie said. "I want to visit with Mandy and see where you're having the ceremony."

Berkley rolled her eyes and nudged me with her shoulder. "In mom speak, that means she wants to see if I've forgotten anything."

Marjorie ignored the comment by pressing her lips into a thin line. "First, I'd like to see my son. I know Reese is busy, but surely he can spare some time for his mother."

Even though I knew Reese was keeping his father busy, I'd secretly yearned to see him, at least one more time—alone. After tonight, things were going to be hectic. The wedding was tomorrow, I'd be working long into the evening, and the day after that, I'd planned to leave.

Not seeing him was probably for the best. He'd be

angry once he found out how I planned to spend my evening, the parting gift I decided to give Berkley and her family. If everything went the way I hoped, and with a certain bear's help, namely Bryson, I was going to get some photos of the construction thieves. Of course, in order to get the information I needed from Bryson, I'd had to bribe him by offering to take additional pictures of him and Leah after the reception.

He'd tried to persuade me into returning to do their wedding after they'd set a date, but I'd declined. It would be too hard and unfair to my cat if I had to come back and face Reese again once I left.

"Mom, there's something you need to know." Berkley's mother was the only person I knew that could make my friend's grimace look utterly painful. Since she'd also gone pale, I was pretty sure whatever she was going to say had something to do with Clayton's visit.

"Oh, you mean that your father is staying at the lodge and plans to attend the wedding?"

"How did you find out?" Berkley asked.

"Mandy was worried about Nick and called last night to talk," Marjorie said.

"And you're okay with him being here?"

"I'm not thrilled, but it's not going to ruin my visit."

"Are you sure?" Berkley looked like she had her doubts.

"Don't worry. Your father might have been a terrible spouse, but we still know how to be civil to each other." Marjorie draped an arm over each of our shoulders. "Now let's go see what else needs to be done for the wedding."

***

REESE

"Where's Clayton?" my mother asked when I took a seat next to her at the table in the employees' kitchen. She wasn't a vindictive person, wasn't prone to exacting revenge, but the glint in her dark eyes made me wonder if her inquiry included some retribution for the past offenses my father had committed.

I'd promised Berkley I would do everything possible to keep my parents apart for the next few days, and I'd meant it.

"I thought it would be better if he ate in the restaurant." During the short time I'd been in the kitchen talking to the cook, my father had befriended some guests who were part of a bus tour, and they'd invited him to join them for dinner. As long as whatever my father did kept him out of trouble and away from my mother, I wasn't going to complain.

After spending the entire day with my father, my penance for not telling Berkley about his visit, I needed a break. Nick hadn't been happy with me either, but at least he wouldn't hold a grudge, not like our sister. There was no such thing as quality time with my father, not when a drive around the property included an extensive update on the construction, the cost involved, and the financial worth of my siblings and me.

He'd asked probing questions, questions outside my comfort level. If my father and I had a better relationship, one built on trust, I'd have been inclined to answer them fully. Instead, I'd avoided most of them by changing the subject.

He'd been impressed with the renovations and changes we'd made since the last time he'd been here, which, if I remembered right, had been back when Berkley and I were teenagers. I had no idea why my deceased grandfather and his son never got along, but whatever the reason, it had resulted in my father being excluded from inheriting any portion of the resort.

By the time we'd returned to the lodge, the sun was setting and I was looking forward to spending some time relaxing with the other members of my family. Most of all,

I wanted to see Jac. With our mating status unsettled, my wolf had been agitated all day. He was riding me hard to find her, to be close to her, to claim her.

I'd taken one look at Berkley and known she'd had a similarly exhausting day with my mother. Besides everything she did to help me run the resort, she'd been working hard to get everything ready for the wedding tomorrow. I'd insisted she take the night off from cooking. Instead of arguing as I'd expected, she gave me a grateful smile. We kept the restaurant in the lodge open longer on Friday and Saturday evenings, so I kept things simple and ordered everyone a burger-and-fries platter from the kitchen.

Our group consisted of my mother, my siblings, their mates, and myself. Bryson and Leah had also been invited to stay at the lodge since they would be helping with final preparations in the morning, but they'd decided to eat in their room. No surprise there. They were newly mated and had a tendency to spend their time with each other.

Thinking about mates reminded me that mine hadn't made an appearance. "Where's Jac? Isn't she joining us?"

"She said she hasn't been sleeping well and had a headache." Berkley snatched a fry off Preston's plate, earning her a growl.

"Is she all right?" Every protective instinct I possessed was screaming that I should check on her. It didn't matter that Jac had refused to accept me—the need to protect, comfort, and see to her needs was overwhelming.

"I told her she needed to go lie down for a while," my mother added. "I'm sure she'll join us later when she's feeling better."

"You could always go check on her if you're worried." Berkley slapped Preston's hand when he retaliated by stealing some of her fries.

"I think I will." I grabbed a bottled water out of the refrigerator, along with her untouched plate, and headed out of the kitchen.

When I reached her room, I listened outside her door, then knocked when I didn't hear anything. "Jac, it's Reese. I brought you something to eat."

No answer, no noise, no nothing.

What if she was hurt and couldn't answer? She'd been adamant about us not being together. What if she'd packed her things and left? My gut clenched, and I rapped hard three more times without getting an answer.

Berkley, Nick, and I had a set of master keys for all the rooms. After setting the plate and the bottle on the floor, I unlocked the door and stepped inside. With my enhanced vision, it didn't take long for my eyes to adjust to the darkness. Her bed was empty, her bathroom door open, the room dark.

I flipped the light switch on the main wall. Her belongings were strewn around the room pretty much the way they'd been the day before. Seeing she hadn't left eased the pressure in my chest.

I was halfway across the room to check the patio for clothes, to see if she'd gone for a run, when I realized her camera bag was missing. I knew exactly what she was doing and where she'd gone. "Damn it, Jac," I growled and wrenched open the patio door. I jumped off the deck and headed into the forest, torn between draping her over my knees to give her one hell of a spanking or torturing her with kisses for making me worry.

CHAPTER TWELVE

JAC

The headache excuse I'd given Berkley had seemed believable. By the time everyone was done eating, I'd hoped it would be late. With any luck, they'd assume I'd fallen asleep and wouldn't bother checking on me. I'd found the perfect hiding spot in a tree with thick branches and plenty of leaves, to observe the construction site without being seen. If this was an inside job as Berkley and her brothers suspected, then whoever was behind the thefts would know that everyone would be preoccupied with tomorrow's wedding.

They might also know there was a security guard posted not far from the site where the new lumber had been delivered. It only made sense the next place they'd hit would be the one Bryson said hadn't been vandalized yet, the one with random patrols.

On the other side of the clearing was a padlocked storage shed containing equipment. I didn't know if the items inside were as valuable as the lumber, but I'd hoped it had enough appeal to attract the thieves. The visibility provided by the two generator-powered lights sitting nearby wasn't ideal, but I'd be able to get some decent shots with my long-range lens.

Even if I was wrong, a night in the woods sleeping in a tree would be more relaxing than spending a frustrating night fantasizing about Reese. At least that was what I thought until I heard growling. Not the low, nonthreatening growl of a nocturnal creature, but the loud, territorial growl of an irate wolf. I leaned to the side and found Reese standing at the base of the tree, hands on his hips, glaring up at me.

"I thought I told you not to get involved, that this is too dangerous."

All shifters were hardwired with the need to protect their mates. Dominant males were the worst. I should have known when I didn't show up for dinner with his family that he'd come looking for me. "And I clearly remember telling you I didn't take orders from anyone, not even you. Besides, I wasn't foolish enough to come out here without telling someone first." Since cell phone coverage in the area wasn't reliable, Bryson made me take a handheld radio with me in case I needed help.

"Who did you tell?" He fisted his hands against his thighs, appearing as if he wanted to strangle someone.

I was obviously at the top of his list, which was why I refused to leave the tree. "It doesn't matter." Reese started listing the names of everyone he could think of while scrutinizing my face for a reaction. You'd think with all the interrogations my father had put me through, I'd be better at masking my emotions. When he got to Bryson, I couldn't stop myself from flinching.

"Bryson knew you were coming out here, *alone*," he snarled, then muttered a few words I couldn't understand. He rubbed the back of his neck and started pacing.

"Not exactly."

He stopped moving and was back to glaring at me. "What do you mean not exactly?"

"In Bryson's defense, I may have insinuated you were

coming with me, so don't you dare yell at him, fire him, or do anything else to him." I knew Bryson planned to spend the night in his room with Leah, so he'd have no reason to check on me, not if he thought I was with Reese. I'd hoped to get the pictures I needed, then get back to my room before anyone knew I'd been gone.

"If I promise not to reprimand Bryson, will you come down?" he asked.

As far as I knew, Reese was an honorable male. If he agreed to my wishes out loud, then I felt confident he wouldn't go back on his word. "Or fire him."

"Fine. I won't yell at, maim, or throttle him. And he can keep his job." He'd softened his tone. "Now will you get out of that tree?"

"Uh. No. Not until I get pictures of the thieves, which isn't going to happen with you down there yelling at me." I smirked. "Why don't you go back to the lodge, and I'll talk to you in the morning."

"Like hell." He grabbed the first sturdy branch he could reach.

So not good. "What do you think you're doing?" I pulled my legs up onto the branch and squatted, then glanced around for a way to escape. Wolves were great on the ground, had no problem making large jumps and leaps. My cat had more flexibility and could easily move from one tree to another.

"There's no way I'm letting you stay out here by yourself." He continued climbing until he'd reached my branch.

Luckily, the one I'd chosen was sturdy enough to hold our combined weight. I put some distance between us and waited to see what he'd do. He straddled the branch, then used the trunk to brace his back.

"We might as well get comfortable." He smiled and held out his hand, motioning for me to sit in front of him.

Bad idea. "I'm fine over here." We weren't even touching, and my cat was purring and kneading her paws, happy to be near him.

"It could be a long night. What happens if you get tired and go to sleep? The way you're sitting, you'll end up falling out of the tree."

I rolled my eyes. "You do know when cats fall, they land on their feet, right?" I'd never told anyone that during my first few shifts I'd landed on my ass and ended up with bruises that made sitting unpleasant. It wasn't something I planned to start sharing now.

"I'm aware." He grinned and patted his thigh. "Come on, I'll even let you use me as a pillow."

It was still a bad idea, but leaning against his firm chest would be more comfortable than spending hours crouching on the branch next to him. "I want you to know I'm doing this against my better judgment." I looped the strap of my camera around my neck, then crawled along the branch and situated myself in front of him.

He wrapped his arms around my waist and pulled me closer. I glared at him over my shoulder and gave him a silent warning to behave himself.

"What?" He feigned innocence. "I have to put them somewhere."

***

REESE

I ignored the rough edges of the tree trunk digging into my back. I'd spend the night sleeping on jagged rocks if it meant having more time with Jac. I kept my triumphant grin to myself after she relented and allowed me to keep my arms wrapped around her. If she'd noticed the erection I was sporting, the one pressing along her spine, she kept it to herself.

"Shouldn't you be back at the lodge refereeing your parents or something?" she asked.

"They'll be fine. My mother's with Berkley and my

father is off doing other things." I hoped those other things didn't include him being unfaithful to Katie. "I'd rather spend time with you." I expected her to tense up and try to wiggle out of my grasp, but she surprised me by relaxing against me.

"Oh yeah, I can see where spending the night with bark poking you in the ass would be a lot of fun." She removed her camera from around her neck. After aiming it at various spots on the site, she made some adjustments, then held it in her lap.

I'd been contemplating the reasons she'd given me for refusing to be my mate. They'd seemed vague, and now that we were alone, I hoped to get some clarification. "Is there a reason you dislike anyone associated with the military?" When she stiffened, I was afraid I'd said the wrong thing, that she'd pull away. "I know it's none of my business, and you don't have to answer unless you want to."

She paused for several moments before speaking. "I spent too many years trying to earn my father's approval." She nervously twisted the strap on her camera. "Everything from learning how to shoot a variety of weapons to taking survival training."

"Are you talking about the courses where you're left in the middle of nowhere and then expected to survive off the land?" Those courses were tough, and I was impressed.

"No, my father wanted a son, so he tried to turn me into a soldier. He sent me to a special shifter camp where they teach you to be part of a team and you learn how to blend in with your surroundings."

"Did you make it all the way through?" I'd heard about the camp. Those who signed up were mostly male and, by nature, would have made it difficult for a female. The training was tough and hard-core, not something I envisioned Jac signing up for, let alone being forced to endure.

"Of course. Doesn't everyone want to have being able

to capture an opponent's flag on their résumé?"

It hadn't escaped me that she used sarcastic humor as a defense mechanism. No wonder she didn't want to have anything to do with me. I was ex-military, a reminder of things from her past that she wanted to avoid. "Jac, I'm…" *Sorry and would like to hurt your father for what he put you through.*

"It's okay." She straightened, her attention trained on the opposite side of the clearing. "Did you hear that?"

I strained to listen, to find the source of the noise, then heard a rumble. "Truck engine."

"I knew it." She bobbed her head proudly.

A few seconds later, the bright beam from the headlights splashed across the area as the vehicle came into view. The driver parked at an angle, which prevented me from getting a good look at the license plate. Two men dressed entirely in black and wearing ski masks got out of the truck. The man who exited on the passenger side was carrying a large bolt cutter and headed straight for the storage shed. The other moved to the rear of the truck and lowered the tailgate.

"You don't have any security cameras out here, do you?" Jac asked.

"No, why?"

"Don't you think it's strange they're wearing masks in the middle of the night?" She swung her legs so they hung off the same side of the branch.

"It's possible they work on one of the sites and didn't want to be recognized if one of my security guys caught them."

"Good point." She held up her camera and aimed. "I know I said I was only going to take pictures, but now that you're here, shouldn't we do something?" She snapped a couple of shots.

I placed my hand on her thigh. "No, we're going to stay right here until they leave."

She narrowed her eyes and frowned. "You're okay with

just sitting here and letting them steal your property?"

"Yes, because I'm not willing to risk either of us getting shot." I didn't want her anywhere near the males and neither did my wolf.

"But they're not armed, and if we can't see their faces, these pictures aren't going to do much good," she argued.

If I'd been alone, my answer about just sitting here would've been no. Being a shifter with military training gave me an advantage. Even if the males had been carrying weapons, I could easily overpower them. At the moment, keeping Jac safe was my priority. I didn't have to ask her to know she wouldn't stay hidden in the tree and let me take care of the males.

"Doesn't matter. Some of the people who live on the mountain like to hunt, and there's a good chance they have weapons inside the truck." I had no way of knowing if these two males, wolf shifters if I was scenting correctly, resided anywhere near the resort. I wasn't going to put Jac's life in jeopardy if I was right.

"Sorry, but I'm not a sit-back-and-do-nothing kind of girl." She elbowed me in the ribs hard enough to make me loosen my grip on her leg. She pushed away from me, and in the sleekest move I'd ever seen a female make, she looped the strap of her camera on one of the smaller branches above our heads, then sprang to the next tree, her movement silent, graceful, precise.

"Damn stubborn female," I snarled under my breath. Surely she had to know this was dangerous, and it sure as hell wasn't the same as trying to capture another team's flag.

She had the audacity to stop and wink at me before leaping to the next tree. I wasn't going to let her face the males alone. I pushed aside my anger and quickly formulated a plan. Wolves weren't designed to play in the trees; we were better on the ground. I shoved away from the branch and landed easily on my feet without making a sound. Staying in the shadows, I used the trees for cover, then raced to the other side of the clearing, hoping I'd get there before she did.

***

JAC

The furrowed brows and the hard line along Reese's jaw had me convinced he was ready to strangle me. I probably shouldn't have winked, but I couldn't help myself. I knew his anger stemmed from his wolf's need to protect me. What I wanted—no, *needed*—was his human side to understand I wasn't a fragile female and could take care of myself. Mostly, I wanted him to know I had an independent nature and needed him to support me, not try to control me.

By staying in the treetops, it didn't take me long to reach the tree closest to the males' truck. I leaped into the air and landed with a loud thud on the hood of the cab. "You boys want to tell me what you're doing?"

The males, both wolves, jerked their heads in my direction. Their dark masks hid their faces, but from this distance, I could see the angry glint in their eyes. One pair was brown, the other green.

"Who the hell are you?" Mr. Green Eyes asked, then dropped the toolbox he'd taken from the shed on the end of the tailgate.

At the same time, the male with brown eyes reached for the bolt cutters he'd set on the ground and propped against the building's exterior.

"I could ask you the same thing. I'm pretty sure you're trespassing." I glanced at the toolbox, then back at the males. "And stealing from the resort."

"Fuck, John." Green Eyes glared at his buddy. "I told you this was a bad idea, that it was only a matter of time before we got caught."

"Shut up, you idiot, and stop using my name. You know what he'll do to us if we don't finish the job." John gripped the bolt cutter tighter, his voice cracking with fear.

Based on his comment, it didn't take a genius to know these two were lackeys, that there was someone else organizing the thefts. Someone who didn't do his own work and made sure others would be blamed if anything went wrong.

I scented Reese, then out of my periphery got a glimpse of him moving through the shadows, inching toward the right side of the truck. Once these two stopped arguing, it wouldn't take long before they detected his odor. I wasn't sure what he planned to do, but decided a distraction couldn't hurt.

"Hey, guys, do you mind telling me who you're talking about? Who's in charge of your operation?" I didn't think they'd give me the other male's name. They appeared to be more afraid of him than they were of me.

The only acknowledgment I got was a seething glare from both men.

"What are we going to do with her, Mick?" John asked. "I saw her at the site with Reynolds. We can't let her leave. The boss will kill us when he finds out someone saw what we were doing."

"Now that she's seen us and knows our names, we'll have to take her with us," Mick said.

"He's not going to like it."

"He doesn't have to know. She's one puny female. There's plenty of places on the mountain where we can get rid of her so no one will find her," Mick said.

Puny, seriously? Having males underestimate my abilities was nothing new. My cat was stretching her claws, eagerly urging me to correct their assumption.

"Fine, hurry up so we can get out of here before someone comes looking for her," John said.

"Why don't you climb down off there so we can talk?" Mick hopped up on the tailgate and sidestepped the toolbox.

It appeared they were limited on brain cells as well. "What am I, five years old? I just heard you tell your friend you planned to make me disappear." I shook my head and flexed my fingers. "Not a brilliant move on your part."

If I could keep them talking, they'd be too distracted to shift. Because of my cat's size, fighting would be more difficult and bloody. It wouldn't be the first time I'd battled a larger animal. I was more concerned about Berkley's reaction if I showed up at the wedding covered with scrapes and bruises. Minor injuries would disappear in a few hours; anything deeper would take a lot longer.

Mick snarled and dove at my legs. I jumped straight up latching on to an overhanging branch and narrowly missed his lunge. His miscalculation caused him to overshoot his reach and smack the metal surface with his chest.

"Jac, get out of here," Reese yelled as he rushed at John and tackled him from behind. John grunted. The bolt cutters flew through the air and bounced off the shed. At the same time, Reese and John hit the ground, and I lost sight of them.

"Not without you." I was overwhelmed by the need to help Reese, to protect my mate. I wasn't going to seek safety, nor was I going to give Mick a chance to go after him. I whipped my legs through the air and released my grip, performing a perfect somersault and landing on Mick's back. I dug my newly extended claws into the muscles on his shoulders and wrapped my legs around his hips.

"Get off me, bitch." He shoved to his feet, spinning in a circle, his boots thudding on metal as he tried to dislodge me from his back. I dodged the sharp claws he swiped at my face, then bit the side of his hand when it got close to my mouth.

He banged my lower back against the frame of the rear window. Pain radiated along my side, and I groaned. I refused to let go and dug my nails in deeper, his blood soaking the shirt beneath my fingertips.

He screamed, lost his footing, and toppled over the side of the truck's bed. Unfortunately for me, he twisted at the last second, his larger body landing on top of me, forcing the air out of my lungs with a heavy whoosh.

I choked and coughed, the need for air stronger than the need to keep my claws firmly in place. Mick rolled and was on me in seconds, straddling my waist, his fingers wrapped around my throat. I clawed at his wrists, scraping skin, trying to get free. He was too strong, the pressure on my neck too great.

Reese was nowhere to be seen, and all I could think about was whether or not my bold decision to engage the males had caused him harm or gotten him killed. Not that it mattered now. Not at the rate my vision was blurring, my body spiraling closer to unconsciousness and possibly death.

A feral, agonized growl ripped through the air. An instant later, Mick was wrenched away from me. I heard a loud bang accompanied by the crackle of breaking bones.

"Are you all right?" Reese was on his knees at my side. "Where are you hurt?"

He grimaced, then cupped the side of my face and tipped my chin to examine my neck, which was probably covered with red marks. He brushed his fingertips over the painfully tender area, his touch gentle and caring.

"I'm okay." I reassured him by placing my hand over his. I was relieved not to see signs of injury on him.

"Promise me you won't ever do that again." He sat back in the dirt and pulled me onto his lap.

It was a promise I couldn't make, so I remained silent and let him cradle me against his chest, the action soothing for both our animals. I lifted my head and held his gaze. "Reese, I…" My apology was swallowed by his kiss. A devouring kiss, an intermingling of mouth and tongue so possessive that it left me breathless and panting.

When he finally pulled away and my pulsing heart

slowed enough for rational thought, I whispered, "Thank you for helping me."

"You're welcome." He groaned and lifted me off the ground, keeping an arm around my waist until I could stand on my own. "I suppose arguing or telling you I told you so wouldn't do any good, would it?"

"Probably not."

"Have you always been so strong-willed and stubborn?"

I took his smile as a good sign. "Pretty much."

He shook his head, defeated. "We should be getting back."

I glanced to my left and spotted Mick and John unconscious in the dirt, a result of Reese's impressive handiwork. "What are we going to do about them?"

He pulled his cell out of his back pocket and stared at the screen. "With no service and without cell reception, we won't be able to get anyone out to the site, including the police."

The radio Bryson had given me was in my bag. I didn't mention it because I didn't want to interrupt his evening with Leah. "Couldn't we take their truck and use the landline back at the lodge?"

"Not a bad idea." He grinned and tweaked my chin.

"Do you think whoever they're working for will come looking for them?"

"It's possible." He grabbed the toolbox off the tailgate and carried it into the shed, returning a few seconds later with some rope. "We'll take them with us just in case."

"I'll be right back. I need to get my camera," I hollered over my shoulder, already sprinting toward the tree where we'd been hiding.

When I returned, Reese had finished securing Mick's and John's hands and feet with the rope. He picked them up one at a time and not so gently tossed them on the bed of the truck.

I climbed into the passenger seat of the truck and

waited for him to join me. "Well, that was fun." I hoped a little humor would alleviate the tension I sensed radiating from Reese.

"How was that fun?" He furrowed his brows. "You got hurt."

He knew as well as I did the marks would be gone by tomorrow, that my shifter body would heal the marks long before they turned into bruises. "I know it didn't go as well as I'd hoped, but now you're a lot closer to finding out who's behind the thefts."

He grunted and started the truck. "Is that your way of saying I was right and you should have listened to me?"

I flashed him a wry smile, then snapped my seat belt into place. "Not even a little."

CHAPTER THIRTEEN

REESE

After three strong cups of coffee, the caffeine pumping through my veins had worked its way through my haze of exhaustion. It had been late when Jac and I returned to the lodge, then waited for the Hanford police to arrive and take John and Mick to jail. It was even later by the time I'd explained to my siblings and their mates what had happened at the construction site. Thankfully, my parents had already retired and I didn't have to suffer through their extensive questioning or listen to any parental lectures.

While we'd waited for the police, Preston and I had done some interrogating of our own. We'd learned the males worked on the framing crew, but they'd refused to give up the identity of the man responsible for masterminding the thefts. Whether they'd meant to or not, they'd given me an obscure detail that might lead to the location of my stolen property. During one of their many arguments, Mick made an offhanded remark, referring to the nickname for an area on the mountain that only someone who'd grown up here would know anything about.

I adjusted the blinds on the patio door to let in more of the early afternoon sun, then pushed aside my concerns and focused on the day's event.

"Explain to me again why tying this thing around my neck is important." Nick walked out of my bathroom tugging on the ends of the tie draped beneath the collar of his white shirt. Keeping with the groom-not-seeing-the-bride-before-the-wedding tradition, he was using my room to shower and dress. I wasn't sure why Mandy thought it was important since they'd spent the previous night alone in their cabin.

I understood his frustration. It had been some time since I'd worn any kind of suit, military or otherwise. My wolf didn't like the constricting clothing either, but did his best to tolerate them.

Berkley had stellar taste when it came to fashion. She'd done an excellent job selecting Nick's outfit. It was the first time I'd seen him wearing anything besides a T-shirt, jeans, or sweats. He had yet to put on his shoes and socks. My brother would go barefoot all year if I hadn't insisted he keep his feet covered around the human guests and employees.

"Because you want to make your mate happy." I took the ends of the silky material and folded them so they would slide easily into place. "And you need to look presentable in your wedding photos." Thinking about the pictures we'd be posing for later reminded me I hadn't seen Jac since shortly after we'd returned to the lodge. She'd conveniently escaped to her room before having to answer any of my sister's questions.

I'd heard her leave her room early this morning and hadn't heard her return. If I didn't already know that she was down at the cabin with Berkley and my mother helping Mandy get ready, I'd be worried that she was sneaking around doing something I'd warned her not to.

"Speaking of photos, how's it going with Jac? Has she agreed to let you claim her yet?" Nick wiggled his brows.

Jac's refusal to accept me as her mate and my nosy family's comments on the topic continued to rub my nerves raw. "None of your business." I adjusted the tie under his collar a little tighter than necessary.

"That's a 'no,' then." He growled, smacked my hand away, then worked the tie loose so he could breathe better. "You should talk to…"

I knew what he was going to say and held up my hand. "Save it. I already got the same advice from Preston. I'm not asking Mandy and Berkley for help."

"You might change your mind if Jac decides to leave after the wedding." He opened the closet, took his suit coat off a hanger, and put it on.

A wave of panic tightened my chest. "What are you talking about?" I knew she might leave, but I'd convinced myself that I had more time, that I'd be able to get past her preconceived views about the kind of male I was and win her over.

"Just that I overheard Berkley talking to Mandy. She said Jac keeps evading the question, hasn't accepted the photographer job yet. Berkley's afraid she's not going to stay."

There was a loud rap, then the door leading into the hallway opened. "Hey," Preston said as he walked inside. I never understood why the damned cat couldn't wait to be invited into a room before he entered. "Berkley wants to know if you two are ready?" He glanced at Nick's feet and grinned. "You planning on going barefoot?" Preston strolled across the room and leaned against the dresser with his legs crossed at the ankle.

"Damn, I forgot." Nick plopped on the edge of the bed, then pulled a pair of black suede shoes and dark socks out of his duffel bag. He glanced at Preston and said, "Since you're here, maybe you can talk some sense into my idiot brother. You know Berkley will find a way to blame us and make our lives hell if Jac leaves." He finished slipping into his shoes, then stood and adjusted the belt on his pants.

Preston frowned and pushed away from the dresser. "Seriously, Reese. You need to make this right before Nick and I end up sleeping on the floor."

I glared at my soon-to-be-ex-friend. "You're my sister's mate, so I understand why you'd be concerned. But I don't see how this will affect Nick."

"Because if Berkley is upset, she'll tell Mandy, then the two of them will…" Nick shook his head.

I rubbed a hand down my face. "Are you saying the fate of your sex lives hinges on whether or not I claim Jac?"

"Yes." They bellowed their emphatic response simultaneously.

***

Berkley had done a great job turning one of the lodge's meeting rooms into a chapel complete with a wide aisle down the middle of two chair-filled sections. If the bridal packages she was developing were profitable, we'd eventually build a separate chapel to accommodate bigger groups. During several of our marketing discussions, she'd also talked about building a gazebo for couples interested in having their weddings outside.

I peeked through the partially opened door leading into a larger area where the actual ceremony would take place. The room was filled with family, employees, and the people from town who were either close personal friends or those we did business with. There were a lot of people, human and shifter alike, who liked and respected Nick and Mandy.

Bryson had been assigned usher duties and was busy escorting the new arrivals to their seats. I noticed he'd seated my parents on opposite sides of the aisle, no doubt complying with my sister's explicit instructions.

The bridal party, except for Nick, who was standing

near the makeshift altar inside the chapel, was nervously waiting for the ceremony to begin. I had to give my brother credit. Wild wolves had a natural aversion to crowds. It took a lot of effort to control his wolf around this many people. It also showed how much he loved his mate.

I closed the door and went back to pacing, eager to get things moving. After Nick had dropped the Jac-might-be-leaving bomb, I was even more anxious to see her. My wolf was going nuts. If Berkley hadn't made it a point to let me know Jac would be arriving shortly, I would have gone to the cabin and dragged her here myself.

Roy Jensen, Mandy's father, slipped into the room behind me. "Hey, Reese." He patted my shoulder, then headed straight for his daughter. He took her hands, gave her an admiring look, then pressed a soft kiss to her cheek. "You look so beautiful, sweetheart."

"Thanks, Dad." She smiled and squeezed his hands. "Is Barb coming?"

Mandy's mother had passed away when she was young. Barb was her father's widowed next-door neighbor who had been their friend for years and was currently the love of his life.

"She wouldn't miss it. She's already inside saving me a seat," Roy said.

Mandy hadn't wanted anything fancy and kept the bridal party small. Roy was there to give her away. Preston was paired with Berkley, and I was paired with Nina.

A click of heels coming from the hallway next to the open doorway on the opposite side of the room drew everyone's attention. A few seconds later, Jac appeared with her camera bag slung across her right shoulder. Her gaze locked with mine as she gave me the briefest of smiles, before shifting her attention to the others in the room. "How is everyone doing?"

She'd looked gorgeous in the sundress she'd worn two nights ago, but it had nothing on the dress hitting midthigh and accentuating her petite frame. Thin straps exposed her bare shoulders, and the sheer black fabric with a floral print matched her garnet eyes. I couldn't stop staring, my mouth was hanging open, and no matter how hard I tried, I couldn't move my jaw muscles.

"Nervous, but great," Mandy answered with a beaming smile.

"I can't thank you enough for doing this for us." Berkley walked over to Jac and gave her a quick hug.

"It's my pleasure." Jac set her bag on the floor, then retrieved her camera and glanced around the group. "I know we talked about this before, but I wanted to remind everyone that I'll be taking pictures during the ceremony, then immediately afterward, I'll start taking the group photos."

It took a cough and Preston's elbow in my ribs to get me to realize there was music playing in the background, signaling the start of the wedding. I vaguely recalled getting in line to escort Nina down the aisle before taking my place next to Nick. The actual ceremony was a blur.

My thoughts, my focus, my wolf, were lost in watching Jac as she worked her way around the outskirts of the room snapping the occasional picture. The attraction between us came with being her mate, but for me, it was a lot more. Sometime over the last few days, I'd fallen for her. My heart ached, knowing if I didn't do something drastic to change her mind, I was going to lose her forever.

***

JAC

I hovered near a corner table, listening to the low drone of music and watching everyone enjoy themselves. The wedding had been simple, with a touch of country elegance. Berkley had done an outstanding job. She'd transformed the restaurant's dining room into a reception hall complete with a portable dance floor. I had no doubt the wedding packages she was putting together were going to be successful. I was disappointed I'd never get to be a part of it. Worse was the deep regret, the ache bearing down on my heart every time I thought about walking away from Reese.

As the best man, he was in a majority of the photos, making it nearly impossible to concentrate. He made a pair of jeans look good, but damn if he wasn't an impressively handsome male in the white shirt and black suit he was wearing. A suit I wanted so badly to remove from his body. The need to be with him, to mate, to claim, was getting stronger the longer we were together.

Logic continually battled with my emotions and my increasing attraction to Reese. The fact that I cared about him and thoroughly enjoyed his company, dominant nature and all, didn't help with the lingering doubts I had about my decision.

All I had to do was think about my controlling father and the years I'd wasted trying to gain his approval. With every disdainful grimace, every disappointed sneer, every condescending remark, he'd reminded me that no male would want a hybrid as a mate. I was an anomaly, a rarity in the shifter world, a cat that had taken on the feline traits of both of my parents as well as a domestic cat hidden somewhere several generations back in my lineage.

Reese might be able to accept my animal, but what happened if we had children and the rare gene made an appearance? Would he love and protect them, or would he treat them as rejects the same way my father had treated me? Would he regret his decision to take me as a mate and gradually grow to hate me? I would rather be alone forever than risk seeing a hateful look in his stunning eyes.

"Dance with me." Reese appeared behind me, pulling me from my troubled thoughts. His whisper, a warm caress, sent chills racing along my bare shoulder.

I took a moment to enjoy his hand on my hip, to savor

his masculine scent before turning to face him. "I don't think that's a good idea. I'm working."

"Since I know the owner personally, I'm sure he won't have a problem with you taking a break." He lifted the camera out of my hand and tucked it into my bag, which I'd placed on the floor under the table in the corner. "I'll even let you lead."

"You might change your mind when I start stepping on your toes."

"A little embarrassment never hurt anyone." He took my hand and tugged me toward an empty spot in the middle of the floor.

The warmth from his hand seeped through the thin material covering my lower back. "Was that an attempt to be charming?"

He widened his eyes. "Is it working?"

Yes. "No, not even close."

He released an exaggerated sigh. "Seriously? Because I even practiced in front of a mirror."

I laughed and patted his shoulder. "Poor baby. You'll have to try a different method."

"Really." He gave me one of his heart-melting grins.

His gaze glistened with mischief and dropped to my mouth. My heart raced, and I parted my lips in anticipation of a kiss. A kiss that never came.

"Berkley told me you turned down the job and were planning to leave in the morning." His voice lacked any emotion. No anger. No disappointment. Simply stating a fact.

The tightness in my stomach grew to the size of a medium-sized rock. My body tensed, first because I was disappointed his lips weren't on mine, and second because I'd done my best to avoid this conversation. Once the wedding was over, I didn't think it was right not to tell Berkley about my plans.

"I was hoping you wouldn't mind sticking around one more day," he said.

"Why?" I was confused. Why was he acting like me not taking the job wasn't a big deal, like he didn't care we were mates and I was leaving? What had changed since last night? Had he finally given up? And why did it feel as if someone had used their claws to leave large gashes across my heart?

"I need to follow up on a lead I got from Mick and John. I thought you might want to be included."

Any other time, I would've been thrilled to be asked for my help, but all I felt was upset and hurt. Heavy on the hurt. "I guess one more day won't make any difference."

"Great. Dress comfortably for a day outside and be ready to leave by seven." The song we'd been swaying to ended, replaced by a faster beat. He took my hand and led me back to where he'd found me. After pressing a kiss to my forehead, he walked across the room to stand with Preston.

Too shocked by what had just happened, all I could do was stand there and stare at his back. My cat growled and flexed her claws, exceedingly annoyed by Reese's sudden indifference to us.

"Hey, feel like taking a few more pictures?" Berkley tapped my shoulder and interrupted my thoughts. "I'm not sure how long my parents will be nice to each other, so now might be the only time you can get some pictures of them with Mandy and Nick."

"Sure." I fished my camera out of the bag and draped the strap around my nape. "I'm right behind you."

CHAPTER FOURTEEN

JAC

Glimpsing moments of life through a lens was a rewarding job, but it also meant I spent a lot of time on my feet. It had been a long day and an even longer night, one with little to no sleep. It had been nearing midnight by the time the reception ended and I'd returned to my room.

My dance with Reese was the last time I'd spent any time alone with him. I'd gone from fantasizing about getting him naked to analyzing every possible scenario as to why there was a sudden change in the way he treated me. I should be happy he'd finally given up and was no longer pursuing me as his mate. Instead, I was miserable that I was leaving.

Not surprisingly, Reese had rapped on my door promptly at seven. I'd barely had time to roll out of bed, zip up my jeans, and get a T-shirt tugged over my head before his pounding became more insistent. He'd kept conversation light and to a minimum. Apparently, he wasn't any better at early morning social engagements without a caffeine inducement than I was. After plying me with some much-needed coffee and two of Berkley's humongously delicious cinnamon rolls dripping with icing, he'd led me to his truck.

I wasn't familiar with the outlying roads near the resort, so I didn't question Reese about the lead he'd mentioned or where we were going. Not until we'd reached a place where a large wooden sign was mounted between two round posts on either side of a graveled drive. The words "Gabe's Trail Rides" were carved into the thick grain. The letters were painted dark blue and outlined in yellow. I knew Gabe Miller owned the property next to the resort. I'd seen the brochures advertising his scenic horseback rides, along with pamphlets for other local businesses, on a rack in the lobby. I'd also gotten a brief introduction to the male during the reception the night before.

"This lead that you mentioned... Do you think the thief is one of your neighbors?" I asked.

"No, but we need to stop here first to pick up a couple of things for our trip."

"Are you going to tell me what those things might be?" His evasiveness wasn't helping my anxiety and neither was his annoying grin.

"You'll see." He parked in an empty space next to several other vehicles in a small graveled lot near the side of a large barn.

I got out of the truck, manure the first strong scent I smelled. I was glad I'd decided to wear an old pair of jeans and hiking boots. Gabe's horses weren't selective about where they left their presents, and I had a few near misses as I followed Reese toward the front of the barn.

We reached the main entrance just as Gabe was securing the gate on one of the stalls. He was fit for a man in his late fifties and the cowboy attire, complete with a tan hat, suited him.

"Morning, Reese." He flashed a warm smile, then nodded. "Jac."

"Good morning," I said, still wondering what Reese needed to get from Gabe.

"The saddlebags have everything you asked for," Gabe said.

"Saddlebags." I jerked my head back and forth between Gabe and Reese. "What do we need saddlebags for?"

"For your ride." Gabe tipped his head toward the two horses tied to a nearby fence. One of the animals, slightly larger than the other, was a sleek, shiny black. The one standing next to it was a chestnut brown with a white spot on its forehead. Both of them were fitted with saddles complete with the leather bags he'd mentioned, hanging on either side of their rumps.

I gaped at Reese, unable to form words.

"I'll be back in a few minutes. I need to check on a tour that's getting ready to leave." Gabe acted as if he couldn't get away from us fast enough and sprinted in the opposite direction.

Reese ignored my irritated glare, took my hand, and pulled me toward the beasts. Beasts that got considerably bigger the closer we got.

The man had truly lost his mind. I jerked my hand out of his and took a step backward. "You're kidding, right? There's no way I'm getting on one of those hay-chomping things."

"What happened to no fear?" He crossed his arms, tipping his head slightly to one side, his tone challenging.

"I was talking about mountain climbing, bungee jumping, maybe even alligator wrestling. Not riding on an animal that might decide to toss me off its back, then stomp the living crap out of me." I was being serious, and all he could do was laugh. I considered knocking him on his ass, preferably so he'd land in one of the many piles of horse crap littering the ground near his feet. Lucky for him, Gabe picked that moment to return.

"You'll be perfectly safe. Rosie is one of the gentlest mares I own." Gabe ran his hand along the horse's neck. "And Trapper is a good trail lead."

I wasn't ready to relinquish my doubts. "If you say so."

As if on cue, the animal nudged me with her nose and snorted. Gabe reached into his pocket and pulled out something that looked like a dog biscuit. He held his palm out flat and waited for Rosie to snatch it out of his hand.

"Horse snack," Gabe answered before I could ask.

I remembered how well Bear behaved for Nick after he fed the dog a similar bone-shaped treat. Maybe the same thing applied to horses. "I don't suppose you have a bag of those we could take with us, do you?"

"We won't need them." Reese untied the reins from the fence. "Time to go."

I liked animals, and for the most part, they liked me. I wouldn't back down from the challenge no matter how badly I wanted to. "And how do you propose I get up there?" I pointed at the top of Rosie's back.

"Grab the saddle horn, put one foot in the stirrup, then pull yourself up." He grinned and glanced at my backside. "Unless you'd like me to give you a boost."

As much as I'd enjoy having Reese's hands on my ass, I wasn't going to give him the satisfaction. "I can manage."

Thanks to my cat's agility, mounting was easier than it appeared. Once I was comfortably seated, Reese handed me the reins.

"It's a beautiful day for a ride but I'd keep an eye on the weather." Gabe motioned toward a tiny cluster of storm clouds gathering along the horizon in the distance.

"Will do." Reese hoisted himself up onto Trapper.

I had yet to see him do anything where he seemed out of his element. I'd never had a thing for cowboys, but after staring at those firm, thick thighs and the way his rear filled the saddle, I could easily see the fascination. The view was a definite perk, and maybe this wasn't going to be as bad as I thought.

Of course, after bouncing around on the hard leather surface for a few minutes, I was convinced that Reese had intentionally devised another plan to torture me. I was also sure I'd have sores in unpleasant places by the end of the ride.

It took almost an hour for me to feel comfortable enough with Rosie and her easy gait to relax the white-knuckle grip I had on the horn and enjoy the scenery around us. "Darn it," I said, remembering I'd left my camera sitting in Reese's truck. I'd been so worried about riding that I'd completely forgotten to retrieve it.

Reese turned slightly in his saddle to look back at me. "Is there a problem?"

"I forgot my camera, and I hate missing out on these great shots."

"I'd have been happy to bring you back out here, but you said you needed to leave tomorrow." His voice possessed the same nonchalant tone he'd used during our dance.

"Yeah, I guess," I mumbled, confused more than ever by the comment that tore at my heart and made my cat's meow sound like a whine.

***

"Are you going to tell me where we're going?" What I really wanted to ask Reese was how much longer he expected my poor body to take a beating. Judging by the position of the sun, I assumed we'd been riding a couple of hours. I had no idea where we were, and I had yet to see anything that resembled a trail or any evidence of civilization.

He glanced over his shoulder and grinned. "We're almost there."

The trees began to thin and opened up into a clearing. At the opposite end of the area was a beautifully constructed cabin. The wooden exterior was worn and showed minimal signs of abuse caused by extreme changes in the weather.

"This was your lead?" I glanced around, looking for a stack of lumber or anything else that belonged on a construction site.

"Sort of." Reese stopped his horse, then slid easily from the saddle.

He walked over to Rosie and held the leather strap along the side of her head and waited for me to dismount. Once my feet were firmly planted on the ground, I hooked a thumb at the horses, who had their noses buried in a half-foot-high patch of weeds and wild grass. "Aren't you afraid they'll take off?"

"They'll be fine. Come on, there's someone I'd like you to meet."

"Oh, okay." I hesitantly glanced at Rosie one more time, then took Reese's offered hand and let him lead me toward the cabin.

He had his other hand raised and ready to knock when the door opened. Standing near the entryway was an older male who towered over Reese by at least four inches. He scented of bear and had a silvery beard that reached the middle of his chest. He wore a pair of blue suspenders over an orange plaid shirt with sleeves rolled to the elbows. He reminded me of a hermit or a hermit-type lumberjack.

"Reese, heard you were back. 'Bout time you came for a visit," the old guy said in a chastising tone, then moved away from the door so we could enter.

The interior was an open living space with a kitchen area on the left. The living room started in the middle of the room and expanded into the area on the right. A set of stairs on the back wall led to an overhead loft, which I assumed was used as the bedroom.

"Jac, this is Bart," Reese said once we were inside. "He's the oldest and most cantankerous person living on the mountain."

"Funny name for a female," Bart said.

I'd just met Bart and didn't know anything about him. I wasn't inclined to explain the reason for the nickname I'd chosen to use since high school.

Bart responded to my silence with a huff, then walked

over to a single-door refrigerator sitting at the end of a short counter and pulled out three bottles of beer. After handing one to each of us, he twisted the top off his bottle and took a long swig. "Something wrong with your parents?"

I assumed since he knew Reese that the question was directed at me. "My mother, no." I had fond and loving memories of her up until she'd died. "My father, an undeniable yes."

Reese shook his head. "Sorry, Jac, I forgot to mention Bart's also the *nosiest* shifter in the area."

Bart's lip twitched, the comment clearly taken as a compliment.

A loud blaring chime filled the room, but Bart didn't budge and acted as if he hadn't heard it.

"Wait, you have a phone?" I tipped my head to the side and found the source of the noise sitting on a shelf behind him. "That means Reese could have called you."

Bart shrugged. "Yep. The granddaughter had it installed last summer."

Reese leaned against the kitchen counter and grinned as if a high-security secret was about to be revealed. "Would you have answered it if I'd called?"

"Nope. Why would I?" Bart said and took another swallow.

"So people can reach you without having to come all the way out here." I rubbed my sore backside, getting more irritated by the second.

"I made it my whole life without using them fancy devices. Not gonna start now." Bart tugged on his beard. "Besides, if I talk on the phone, no one comes out to visit."

Bart made an excellent point, and abrasive or not, I found myself liking the old guy.

"I'm guessing you didn't make the trip just so you could introduce me to your female. Want to tell me what I can help you with?"

Reese's female. If only Bart knew how untrue that statement had become. I downed the remainder of my beer in one swallow.

"I've had some lumber and equipment go missing. Have you seen or heard any unusual traffic in the area?" Reese asked.

"Now that you mention it, I did see some trucks comin' and goin' the last couple of days. You might want to check out that old cabin south of here that yer sister and you used to play in when you were youngins."

"Thanks. I think we will." Reese tossed his empty bottle in the tall plastic trash can standing on the far side of the refrigerator.

"Before you leave, let's go out back." Bart headed for the door on the opposite side of the room. "I finished drying a fresh batch of deer jerky. Berkley will be upset if you don't take some back for her."

"We can't have that." Reese chuckled, then placed his hand on my back urging me to go ahead of him.

Outside the back door was a wooden patio that ended in a graveled drive. Sitting about ten feet away under a protective aluminum canopy was a pristine vintage truck. The silver chrome and smooth, spruce-green waxed finish glistened in the sunlight. Everything from the unique headlights to the wide metal grille had been restored. Even the tires had the wide off-white stripes around the rims.

"You have an original 1940 Ford pickup." I'd reached wearing-a-bib level of drooling and couldn't stop myself from shuffling over to admire it. "I love antique vehicles. My mother used to take me to shows when I was a kid."

I held my hand over the finish. "Do you mind if I…" Some owners were temperamental about the touching thing when it came to their classics.

"Not at all," Bart said.

I slid my fingertips along the smooth surface.

"Had it in a show once…took first place." Bart stuck his chest out proudly and hooked his thumbs under his suspenders.

I hunched over to look through the passenger window and tried not to press my nose against the glass. "Wow, is that the original interior?"

"Sure is."

"It's beautiful. Do you ever drive it?" I glanced at Bart and caught Reese grinning at me.

"All the time. Make a trip into town once a week," Bart said.

"Wait a minute." I straightened and turned. "If you go into…" I hadn't noticed the dirt driveway leading through a gap in the trees on the other side of the house when we'd first stepped outside. "You mean there's a road, that we didn't need to ride out here on horses?" I jerked around to face Reese so fast that the muscles in my neck twinged. "Why didn't we drive?"

"Female's gotta point. Why didn't ya?"

"Because I…" Reese pinned Bart with a narrow-eyed glare. "I should go check on the horses." He turned and stomped around the side of the building.

What the heck was Reese up to and why was he being so covert about it? If he thought he could get out of answering the question, he could think again. I'd made it two steps before Bart placed his hand on my arm to keep me from storming after Reese. "I wouldn't be too hard on the boy. I'm sure he had a good reason for doing what he did."

"What makes you think so?" I already knew the reason. Reese was punishing me because I'd refused to be his mate.

"That boy cares about you," Bart said.

"How do you know?" I was more confused than ever by Reese's actions and welcomed any insight.

"It's in his eyes, the way he looks at you. You can be angry with him all you want, but it won't change anything. I think you're making a mistake if you don't give him a chance." He took my hand and squeezed it. "Reese grew up into a fine male despite the problems with his father. If it weren't for James, his grandfather and my best friend, Reese and his sister might not have turned out as good as they did."

Berkley told me they'd spent a lot of their summer vacations at the resort. I always got the impression they were some of the happiest memories from her childhood.

"You're his mate, aren't you?" Bart asked.

I nodded, not sure if he was searching for an explanation.

"You remind me a lot of my Cally. She was headstrong, didn't think we should mate either. Took me a long time to convince her otherwise. Don't regret a day of it."

"Was?"

"She passed away ten years ago."

"I'm sorry." I'd heard that losing a mate, having the bond severed, was more painful than having an organ ripped from your body. Some shifters were never the same afterward.

"Don't be. We got a lot of good years together." His gaze grew more intense. "All I'm saying is it's the differences between you that make you stronger together. Whatever it is that's holding you back, talk to him about it. Let him decide if it's something he can't handle. Don't make the choice for him."

How could I tell Bart that I thought it might be too late, that Reese had already decided he didn't want me?

"You best get going, but before you do…" Bart walked over to the smoker and slid out a tray of thinly sliced meats.

The aroma was wonderful, making my mouth water. He pulled two sandwich-sized plastic bags out of a box, stuffed them with meat, then handed them to me after sealing them. "Stick these in your pocket and make sure you give one to Berkley."

"I will." He was so tall, and I couldn't quite reach his neck, so I settled for giving him a hug around the waist.

"Thank you…for everything."

"Don't forget what I said." Bart gave my hand a hard squeeze, then patted my back. "Now get."

***

REESE

Jac hadn't said much since we'd left Bart's place. I had no idea what they'd talked about when I'd disappeared to avoid answering her question. The longer she remained silent, the more I worried, and the more I wondered if bringing her out here on horseback had made things worse between us.

I pulled Trapper to a stop, giving her time to come up beside me. "There's a great place not far from here where we can stop for lunch before we head back to Gabe's."

Jac tugged on the reins to make Rosie stop next to me, then giggled when the horse followed her command. "You made me ride all the way out here, get blisters in places where a girl should never get blisters, then tell me we're heading back without checking out the cabin Bart told us about first."

I grinned and stared at her thighs. "I'd be more than happy to take care of those blisters for you."

"Hey." She snapped her fingers, drawing my attention away from her legs and back to her cheeks, which were turning the prettiest shade of pink. "You're missing the point."

"I am?"

"Yes, you dragged me out here to follow up on a lead. I'm not going back to the lodge until we've gone to the cabin. So you can either take me there, or I'll wander

114

around until I find it myself." She shook the reins, then frowned when Rosie didn't move. "Just as soon as I figure out how to make these things work."

I'd been partially truthful with Jac the night before when I said I wanted her help on a lead. A trail ride was the only option I could come up with where she'd end up spending all day with me.

After talking to Bart, I didn't want her anywhere near the possibility of danger, but at this point, I was willing to do anything I could to keep her from leaving. "You know, you're really cute when you're bossy." I dug my heels into Trapper's flanks to get him moving, then made a clicking noise to get Rosie to follow.

"You need to teach me how you did that."

"I thought you didn't like the horse, or riding," I said.

"I don't, I mean I didn't. Never mind." She stuck her nose in the air. "Rosie and I are bonding…sort of."

"Lessons will take longer than a few minutes. You plan on sticking around for another day?" I challenged.

"Maybe. I haven't decided." She rolled her eyes at me. "And wipe that smug look off your face."

Her indecision made my heart race faster than it had when I'd finished fighting with John and found Mick strangling her. Was it possible that my plan had worked, that my adventure was wearing down Jac's resolve about not mating? I gripped the reins tightly, doing my best not to show any emotion.

The tension rippling between us had reached a comfortable yet fragile level of trust. A trust I was determined not to ruin by doing or saying anything that might change it. Time passed silently as we wound our way through a copse of thick trees, which eventually leveled off into a meadow.

"Didn't Gabe say something about paying attention to the weather? Please tell me you have a plan to keep us from being caught in the rain." Jac stared at the horizon, which was now covered by a thick wall of ominously dark clouds.

The storm had gotten a lot closer. If I hadn't been so worried about losing her and had been paying better attention, I'd have noticed it had changed direction and was headed right for us. Even if we turned around now and rode back to Bart's, I was afraid we weren't going to make it.

"The cabin's not far from here, but I'm not going to lie. It's going to be close." On a trail without any distractions, Rosie was trained to follow the lead. Jac wasn't an experienced rider and wouldn't know how to handle her horse if she got spooked. I pulled my mount to a stop so the horses were standing next to each other. "We need to move a little faster. I'm going to take your reins, and I want you to hold on to the saddle."

"Okay." The confidence reflected in her gaze was unwavering, and she didn't hesitate to hand me the leather straps.

No sooner had we started moving again when the rain, which moments ago had been a light sprinkle, turned into a heavy sheet of water. In minutes, my clothes were soaked, the fabric of my shirt cold and clinging to my skin.

Lightning lit up the sky, followed by rumbling thunder. The water pooling on the ground quickly turned the dirt into slippery mud. To make things worse, the wind was blowing harder, slapping against my face and making it hard to see.

Branches in the nearby trees swayed, the smaller limbs ripped from the trunks and tossed through the air. I heard a loud crack seconds before an overhead branch snapped and hit the ground in front of me. Trapper spooked and reared, but I managed to stay in the saddle. Rosie jumped sideways, pulling free from my grip. Jac screamed, was thrown from her saddle, and hit the ground hard.

"Jac!" I yelled and dismounted. Another streak of light seared through the sky. Trapper jerked the reins from my hand and bolted into the forest with Rosie following close behind him.

I raced to Jac's side, landing next to her with my knees sinking into the mud. After pulling her into my arms, I pushed the wet hair off her face. "Please tell me you're okay."

"I think so, but…"

"Don't say it." I felt bad enough without being reminded that if we'd taken my truck, we wouldn't be in this predicament.

"Say what? That my suggestion to wrestle an alligator would have been safer?" She forced a smile and let me help her off the ground. "Wouldn't think of it."

She clung to my chest and glanced in the direction the horses had disappeared. "Do you think Rosie will be okay?"

Still shaken by how easily she could have been hurt, I kept my arm wrapped securely around her waist. "They'll head back to Gabe's place."

"How can you be sure?" she asked, her words laced with skepticism.

"Because they're trail horses and can find their way home instinctively."

"Do you think Gabe will send help?" she asked.

"Not in this storm. Some of the roads don't get much use and will have washed out by now." I didn't want her to worry, but I didn't feel good about keeping the truth from her either. "No one will be able to get to us until the storm passes."

During the last lightning strike, the sky had brightened enough for me to get my bearings and know where we were. I took her hand. "Come on, the cabin's not far from here. We can stay there for the night."

"Then what?" Jac shielded her eyes from the rain and stayed huddled next to me, which didn't bother my wolf or me a bit.

"Then we'll find a way to get back to Bart's place. Unless the storm knocked out his phone, we can use it to call Berkley and Nick to come and get us."

***

BERKLEY

"Hey, sweetness." Preston walked up behind me and wrapped his arms around my waist with his broad chest pressed against my back.

"Hey." I smiled, snuggling closer and relaxing into his warmth. I returned to staring out the large-paned windows comprising one wall of the room adjoining the lobby. It gave me a panoramic view of the gradually darkening forest and the bright streaks of lightning along the horizon. The rain was coming down in heavy sheets, and thunder echoed all around us. Occasionally, the lights inside the lodge flickered, and I wondered if we were going to lose power and have to start up the generator we kept out back for emergencies.

My mother was on a flight home. My father had retired to his room. I was glad my parents had managed to make it through the ceremony without shredding each other.

My father had decided to stay a few extra days to spend more time getting to know Nick. Even though he'd told me about Katie and wanting to improve his relationship with all of us, I was still a little leery. It didn't mean I wasn't willing to give him another chance. If my father screwed things up this time, I had three males in my life who would make sure he never did anything to hurt me again.

I loved the hectic chaos that came with running my family's resort, but I was glad the wedding was finally over and all my hard work had been a success. I should be relaxed and enjoying the peaceful calm, yet tension vibrated through every nerve in my body. My thoughts drifted to Reese and Jac. They still hadn't returned, and no one had heard from them.

My brother's plan to follow up on a lead about the construction thefts included getting Jac alone and taking her horseback riding. It didn't include taking a radio so we could reach him. Cell service was intermittent in most areas on the mountain, so they wouldn't be able to call if they ran into trouble. Both of them were capable of handling tough situations, but it didn't stop me from being concerned.

After Nick and I found our mates, I'd worried about Reese. He was always the one who took charge, who took care of everyone else first. He deserved to find happiness. And so did Jac. Her life growing up had been hard, her father even worse than mine.

I desperately wanted to help them, but convincing two equally headstrong people they should be together took a lot of finesse. I also had to abide by the noninterference agreement regarding relationships that Reese and I had come up with in our early teens. Unless he specifically asked for my help, I couldn't interfere. However, there wasn't anything in the rules that said I couldn't use an indirect approach to help the stubborn male, or give Jac and him a nudge to make sure they ended up spending a lot of time together.

So far, my efforts hadn't worked. Jac was planning to leave in a day or two, and there was nothing I could do to stop her. All I could do now was hope the two people I cared about were able to overcome whatever obstacles were keeping them apart.

Light laughter filtered into the room and interrupted my thoughts. I turned my head to see Nick enter the lobby with Bear tucked under one arm and Mandy hanging on the other.

"Aren't you two supposed to be enjoying your honeymoon?" Preston asked.

Mandy scratched Bear's head. "It's a little hard to do anything with this one howling at the storm. Besides, we were hoping you still had some cinnamon rolls left."

"Unless Bryson decided to sneak some home to Leah, there should be a pan in the refrigerator." I didn't mention the extra plastic container I'd stashed under the vegetables in the bottom drawer. I had plans to share them later with Preston when we were alone.

The cell in my jacket pocket chirped with an incoming call, and I jumped more than I should have.

Seeing Gabe's name appear on the screen pushed my anxiety higher. I stepped away from the group to answer the call. "Hey, Gabe. Is everything all right?"

I calmly listened to what he had to say, then thanked him before disconnecting the call. My hand was shaking by the time I slipped the phone back into my pocket.

Preston was perceptive and very good at reading my emotions. He rubbed my arms, then encircled my waist and ran his hands along my spine. "Is there a problem?"

I leaned into his welcoming arms and pressed my palms against his chest. "Gabe said his horses came back without Reese and Jac."

"Do you think something bad happened to them?" Mandy asked, leaning into Nick.

"Maybe they stopped to take a break and the horses got spooked by the storm and took off." Preston continued to rub my back, a relaxing gesture that helped calm my wolf and me. "You know your brother can handle himself in any situation."

Preston and Reese had been stationed overseas together. If anyone knew what my brother was capable of, it was my mate. "I know," I said more to convince myself than the others. Reese was an experienced rider and meticulous in his planning, but even an expert couldn't always be prepared for everything. "Jac is pretty adept as well. Did I mention her father made her take survival training?"

"Isn't that a human thing where they dump people in the middle of nowhere and expect them to survive off the land?" Nick seemed unimpressed since shifters were born with the instincts to survive in the wilderness.

"No, it was more like playing war games where she was part of a team and had to capture her opponent's flag." A nervous giggle escaped my lips when I remembered the night Jac and I had traded stories about our adventures over a six pack of beer and some pizza. "And just so you know, Jac's team never lost." Knowing Reese and Jac were highly skilled when it came to survival wasn't making me feel much better.

"Then they should be fine," Mandy said, rubbing my arm. Besides being an optimist, she was a great friend.

"Don't worry. I'll head out as soon as the storm passes," Nick said.

He was the best tracker I knew, but even he wouldn't be able to find them. There'd been too much rain. The ground was a muddy mess, and their scents would have been washed away a long time ago.

"Reese said they were riding over to Bart's. We'll take one of the four-wheel trucks and start there," Preston added.

A brilliant bolt of light shot through the darkened sky, the thunder booming so loud, the windowpanes vibrated. Bear yelped and jumped out of Nick's arms. He squeezed under the sofa, his nails scraping the hardwood floor.

It was going to be a long night, and I wasn't going to sleep until I knew Reese and Jac were safe. I stared at Bear's quivering tail, the only visible part of his short body, and wondered if he had the right idea.

CHAPTER FIFTEEN

REESE

Jac was lucky she hadn't been injured when Rosie jumped. My wolf was pacing and snarling, overcome with the need to protect his mate. The only thing keeping him calm was having her hand in mine.

Our clothes were soaked and caked with mud. The picnic I'd planned was ruined. The food I'd asked Gabe to pack in the saddlebags had disappeared with the horses. We were stranded in an isolated area of the mountain. The only way my day with her could have gotten any worse was if I'd purposely sabotaged it myself.

The storm had tapered somewhat by the time we reached the cabin. I caught a glimpse of a large pile of lumber—my lumber—stacked close to the side of the building. It was covered with a huge brown tarp, the ends kept in place with ropes that were staked to the ground on all four corners. Later, after the rain stopped, I'd investigate the area. Right now, taking care of Jac was my main concern.

It was unsettling to know someone had recently used the cabin and could still be inside. I hadn't seen any vehicles outside, but that didn't mean the place was empty. I kept Jac behind me as I opened the door and gave the interior a quick survey. Other than the faint lingering scents left behind by John and Mick, the place was empty.

Jac squeezed around me, then sniffed the air. "Darn, all I can smell is Mick and John, and of course some stale beer." She glanced at the empty crushed aluminum cans littering a corner of the floor.

They weren't complete slobs. They'd managed to roll their sleeping bags and stack them in the corner with a couple of folded blankets. Or maybe they were afraid they'd get caught and wanted things ready to go in case they needed to leave quickly.

"After the day we've had, I was hoping we'd find out who was behind the thefts. Oooh, but it was nice of them to leave us a flashlight." She snatched the flashlight off the sill of the window closest to the door. After clicking it on, she aimed the beam around the room.

Thankfully, the structure was sturdy. The windows were covered with a grimy film, but none of them were broken. The floor was dry, and I didn't see any signs of leaking. At least we'd have protection until morning.

Things seemed a little better when the beam bounced off some freshly chopped wood stacked on the floor near the fireplace.

She flashed the light at me, her laugh a combination between a giggle and a snort. "This is killing you, isn't it?"

"No," I grumbled, trying to act indignant and giving up after seeing her perceptively tip her head. "Maybe… Yes. This is not how I'd envisioned our day would go."

"How exactly had you planned for this to go?" Jac walked over to the area designed to be a small kitchen and began opening the lower cabinets and drawers.

"What are you doing?" I asked, changing the subject since I had no intention of explaining my epically flawed plan to get her to change her mind and accept me as her mate.

"Looking for matches since I'm not great at rubbing sticks together to start a fire."

Out of curiosity, I moved around her and opened the upper cabinet that was above her head and out of her reach. "I can't believe these are still here." I held up the box of matchsticks I'd stashed on the shelf years ago.

"You put those there," she said.

"Yeah, when Berkley and I spent our summer vacations with our grandfather, we'd sometimes come here after our runs. Later, when I went through the teenage years where I didn't want to spend time with my sister and Mandy, I'd hang out here with some of the local boys." I grabbed some wood off the stack and squatted in front of the fireplace. "There's some decent fishing spots not far from here."

"Was fishing all you did?"

"Pretty much." I lit a match and worked on getting a fire started.

"Are you sure? Because this looks like a great place to make out. You never lured a female out here with the promise of an adventure?" Jac's humorous tone hinted at jealousy. It gave me hope that the day hadn't been a total waste.

"Nope." I twisted to glimpse her face. "You're the first." *And will be my last.*

Her arousal was immediate, the scent filling the air and making me hard.

She ran her hand through her wet hair. "Oh, I…" It was the first time I'd seen her speechless.

"Why don't you grab the sleeping bags and blankets? We're going to need a place to sleep. We can spread them out in the middle of the floor in front of the fire."

Flames sprang to life, danced around the logs, and cast more light into the room. I stood and turned to find that she'd set the unrolled bags where I'd suggested with the folded blankets on top.

"You should take your clothes off," I said, unable to

resist taunting her.

"What? If you think…no." She crossed her arms and scowled.

I chuckled. "I only meant they'll dry a lot faster if we take them off and drape them on the counter. Here, you can use this to cover yourself." I grabbed a blanket and handed it to her. "But before you say anything, I make no promises about not peeking."

"Fair enough." She grinned, snatched the blanket from my hand, and walked to the other side of the room.

I toed off my boots. They were my favorite pair, but I'd have to replace them. No amount of drying was going to repair the damage they'd suffered from the water. After setting them a short distance from the fireplace, I turned to see that Jac had removed her jacket and shirt. She unclasped her bra, exposing her bare back.

My groan was out before I could stifle it. She was so damned beautiful. I wanted to pull her into my arms and touch every inch of her creamy skin, but I wouldn't make a move until I was absolutely certain she was ready.

Jac jerked her head and gave me an admonishing glare, then reached for the blanket and draped it over her shoulders.

"No promises, remember?" I apologized, my guilt lasting all of a second. I removed the rest of my clothes, then secured the other blanket around my waist, doing my best to hide my erection.

She'd fashioned her blanket like a toga and tucked one end over the other across her chest. After draping her clothes on the edge of the counter, she moved to stand in front of the fire, wearing a wickedly mischievous grin. "So, about that great plan of yours."

***

JAC

Reese had been dodging my question about his reasons for dragging me out here since the first time I'd asked him about it at Bart's. He'd left his radio at the resort. He'd gone out of his way to put us in an environment where he had little or no control. He'd been thoughtful and charming throughout the day. But most importantly, he'd nearly lost it when I fell off Rosie and he thought I'd been injured. Those weren't the actions of a man who didn't care.

I'd been reflecting on his different behaviors throughout the day and had a good idea what he'd been planning. One way or another, I was determined to see if he'd confirm my speculations.

"I wish I'd gotten one of the saddlebags. At least we'd have something to eat." He unzipped the sleeping bags, then spread them on the floor in front of the fireplace by placing them one on top of the other in order to form a single bed.

I remembered the deer jerky Bart had given me. "We do." I reached inside the pocket of my wet jacket and triumphantly displayed the plastic bags, the seals secured, the meat untouched by the rain. "Bart said I was supposed to give one of these to Berkley, but under the circumstances, I think she'll understand." I plopped down in the middle of the makeshift bed with my legs crossed and the blanket covering my lap. I opened the bag and took out a small piece of meat. After taking a moment to savor the aroma, I took a bite. "This is really good."

"Were you going to share those with me?" He sat next to me with his legs stretched out in front of him, then glanced at the bags I protectively clutched in my hand.

"Maybe." I pulled out another piece and waved it in front of him. "But only if you tell me why you made me ride all over the mountain so we could end up here."

He snatched the strip out of my hand. "Technically, you're the one who wanted to see the cabin. I wanted to have lunch, then head back home."

"Yes, but if I hadn't insisted we make the trip, you wouldn't have found your missing lumber." I slipped another morsel out of the bag and answered the inquiring quirk of his brow. "I noticed the tarp when we arrived."

"I brought you out here to prove a point."

"Which is?" I asked.

He took the piece of jerky out of my hand and placed it, along with the bags, on the floor behind him. "That I think you're wrong." His eyes shimmered with longing.

"About what?" I could barely breathe, and the words came out in a rasp.

"About us." He leaned closer and nipped my chin. "About us mating." He brushed soft kisses along my throat. "About letting me claim you." He grazed the sensitive spot on my shoulder meant to bear the bite mark of a mate.

My body was on fire, and it was hard not to whimper. Bart's parting words echoed through my mind. Was the old bear right? Would the differences between Reese and me make us stronger?

Yes, he was organized and controlling, yet after everything we'd been through today it no longer seemed to matter. Was I being unfair by refusing to give him a choice in the decision to mate? My animal was the only obstacle I was unsure about. It would crush me if he couldn't accept her, but I cared about him too much to walk away without finding out how he felt.

I cupped the sides of his face, forcing him to stop and hold my gaze. "We need to talk about my cat."

"I thought she was beautiful. What could possibly be wrong with her?"

"She's a hybrid."

He perceptively narrowed his gaze. "Wait, is she the real reason you don't want to be my mate?"

I took some time to consider his question and realized he'd determined the true source behind my rejection. Everything else was moot, excuses I'd used to make things easier. I swallowed hard, forcing myself to explain, and fearing how he'd react. "My father is a jaguar and my mother was an ocelot. Because I carry a rare gene, I took after my mother...mostly. According to my father, my mother had a relative somewhere in her background that was a house cat. Hence, my fluffy tail."

"It's a gorgeous tail." He held my hand and made small distracting circles with his thumb.

It was getting harder to concentrate. "Yeah, I always thought it was cool until I found out it offended my father. He took my being different as a personal attack on his siring abilities, then forbid me to shift around any of his peers or friends."

"Jac, I don't..."

I placed a finger to his lips. "Before you say anything, I want you to know there is a chance if we mate and decide to have children that the gene could be passed on to them." This was difficult. I inhaled, then puffed out the air before continuing. "They could end up like me, or worse. They could have a wolf's body, a fluffy tail, or who knows what other features."

He pulled my hand away from his mouth and placed a kiss on my palm. "They'd be adorable like their mother and I'd love them as much as I love you."

Firelight reflected in his gaze, desire giving his eyes an amber hue. "Be my mate. Let me claim you." His deep pleading tone touched my soul.

My breath hitched. My insides turned molten. My body ached to be touched. Not just touched, but taken—by him. Reese didn't care that I was different. He actually saw me for who and what I was. And he accepted me.

He was perfect. Perfect in every way possible. Perfect for me. Maybe the goddess of shifter fates knew what she was doing after all.

"Yes," I murmured, then kissed his chin as I straddled his lap. "Yes, I'll be your mate." I ran my hands along his chest, eliciting a groan. I planned to make sure the claiming part was mutually reciprocated and licked the place on his shoulder where I intended to leave my mark.

"Yes, I want you to claim me."

***

REESE

Jac's approval was the only enticement I needed to possessively taste her lips. Over the past few days, I'd gotten glimpses of her naked body. Now that she'd agreed to be mine, I planned to memorize every gorgeous detail. I untucked the end of the blanket and peeled it away from her chest. Starting at the column of her throat, I slowly left a trail of kisses to her breasts. When I sucked a nipple into my mouth and tortured the tip with my tongue, she moaned and arched her back.

The need to be inside her was overwhelming, but I wanted to take my time, to touch every inch of her. Before I plunged my cock into her warm depths and left my mark on her skin, I wanted her teetering on the edge of ecstasy.

I lifted her off my lap and gently placed her on her back. After tearing the blanket from my hips, I settled between her spread thighs. Her eyes sparkled with desire, accented with a golden glow from her cat.

She was perfect. "Mine." A low rumble tore from my chest. I ran my hand across her abdomen, grazing her hip, skimming her inner thigh. She was shuddering and wet by the time I eased two fingers inside her. I pumped slowly and steadily until she was whimpering and grinding against my hand.

"Need you." She tugged on my shoulders, then scraped her small sharp nails along my back.

"I know. I've got you." I removed my fingers and guided my cock to her opening. I was enthralled with the need to mate, to bind us together forever. Heat surged through my blood. Taking her slow was no longer an option. I thrust hard and deep, motivated by her satisfied gasp. I plunged again and again, shifting my hips, trying new angles, learning the ones that made her moan, the ones that increased her pleasure.

I licked the spot I'd chosen to make her mine. "I want forever, Jac."

"Then take it." Her warm breath caressed my skin as she kissed her way down my neck. She sank her cat's sharp fangs into the flesh at the base of my throat, then dug her heels into my buttocks, urging me to thrust into her deeper. She moaned against my skin, her body trembling and writhing from her orgasm.

My body pulsed with pleasurable pain and the urge to complete the bond. I bit on the next thrust, the bite breaking her skin, the taste of her blood exhilarating and hurtling me over the edge.

I wasn't ready to pull out and break the connection, so I collapsed on my back with her lying on top of me and straddling my waist. Our bodies were covered in sweat, our chests heaving.

"That was…" she panted.

"Incredible." I finished, then nuzzled her neck. I felt her tongue rasp over the bite she'd left on my shoulder and realized she was cleaning the wound.

"Is that a cat thing?" It tickled, and I wiggled.

"Maybe… Why?" She gave it several more licks.

"I think it's cute." She had the most amazing ass, and I couldn't help squeezing it.

"Cute, I'll show you cute."

I dodged her swipe by rolling to the side, then encircled

her in my arms with her back pressed to my chest. "And you're adorable." I pressed soft kisses to the back of her neck.

She stopped squirming and giggled. "Adorable works."

I skimmed my fingertip along her hip, tracing the edges of her tattoo. "Beautiful artwork."

"I got it during my younger rebellious days."

"You, rebellious? Never." I laughed as I followed the cat's long tail to the center of her buttocks, then gave the firm muscle a gentle pinch.

"Hey." She glared over her shoulder and smacked my hand.

"Sorry, couldn't resist." I grabbed a couple of chunks of wood and tossed them on the dwindling fire. "Come here." I rolled onto my back and moved my arm so she could use my shoulder as a pillow. "Get some rest." I pinched her ass again. "You're going to need it."

CHAPTER SIXTEEN

JAC

The storm had passed sometime during the night, and sunlight filtered through the cabin window, the bright rays landing on the blanket and warming my feet. The night I'd spent sleeping on the floor tangled in Reese's arms had been the most rest I'd gotten since I'd arrived at the resort. My muscles were stiff, my body aching.

They were good aches, memorable aches, the kind that came from being pleasured numerous times by my mate. The kind I wouldn't trade for anything. I lay on my side with my head braced in my hand. My chest rumbled as I stared appreciatively at his sleeping profile.

Reese opened one eye. "Are you purring?"

"What can I say? My cat is happy." I wasn't embarrassed, and I didn't bother to stifle the low rumble. He rolled on his side so he was facing me.

"And what about you? Are you happy?"

"Oh, yeah." I ran a fingertip over the healing bite mark and smiled. "Extremely happy."

He glanced toward the window and sighed. "I wish we could stay here for the rest of the day, but we really should get going. We don't know who's behind the thefts, and I'd rather not be here if he decides to show up."

"You're not worrying about my safety and doing that overprotective dominant male thing, are you?"

He caught me around the waist and pulled me against his chest before I could escape. "No, I'm doing the protect-my-private-parts-from-my-sister thing, because she'll want to hurt me for making her worry."

"I'd have to agree that saving your manly parts is a very good cause." I laughed and shifted my weight so I was rubbing against his hardened cock. "It's too bad we have to go. It would have been fun to make sure everything was working properly before we left."

He rolled me on my back, settling his hips between my spread thighs. "You never mentioned you had a devious nature."

"I'm your sister's friend. What did you expect?" I raked my nails along his chest.

"I expect to show you just how well my parts work."

***

REESE

An hour and another amazing round of lovemaking later, I finally released Jac and forced myself to get dressed. I kept glancing in her direction, finding it surreal she was my mate, that we'd completed the lifetime bond. She was my future, something to cherish, and I would protect her with my life. My wolf, being the smug animal he was, preened with contentment.

"I want to take a quick look around before we head out," I said as I opened the door. My main concern now was getting her home safely. We came all this way to do some investigating, so I decided to spend a couple of extra minutes checking out the stack of lumber and the area surrounding the cabin. With all the rain, I was certain I wouldn't be able to pick up any additional scents. Maybe I'd get lucky and find another clue to the identity of the person in charge.

"Go ahead." Jac secured the zipper on one of the sleeping bags. "I'll be out as soon as I'm finished rolling these."

Once outside, I circled the cabin, avoiding the worst of the muddy areas until I ended up on the side with the lumber. Hidden behind the stack was another brown tarp draped over a smaller rectangular object and held in place with bungee cords. I unhooked one of the cords and lifted the flap.

Underneath the layer of plastic were several white metal storage containers. The same type I'd seen contractors use in the beds of their trucks. I lifted the lid on the closest one, surprised it wasn't locked. Whoever left the boxes hadn't been concerned they'd be discovered, or they didn't plan to leave them here very long. The box was jammed with expensive tools. Everything from hammers and screwdrivers to a couple of drills and handheld battery-operated saws.

I wondered if there was an illegal market for construction items in the area that I didn't know about. It was one of the first things I planned to research when I got back to the lodge. The other would be talking to the police and seeing if they'd made any headway with Mick and John.

"Wow, did all that equipment come from your sites?" Jac held on to my arm as she leaned forward to peer inside the container.

"I won't know until I check with Bryson and find out what was stolen. There's a chance I'm not the only one being targeted." I lowered the lid, then slipped my arm around her waist and pulled her close. "I hope you're ready for a long hike. I know it would be faster to cut through the forest, but if anyone from the lodge is looking for us, they'll use the access roads."

"What about shifting and going for a run?"

"It would be faster, but not necessarily safer. Occasionally, we get poachers in this area. I don't want to risk it, or you." I didn't think I'd ever get tired of tasting her lips and pulled her close for one more kiss before we left. The moment was cut short by the sound of an engine. I moved to the left to get a better view of the area in front of the cabin and caught a glimpse of red moving through the trees. A few seconds later, I got a better look at the truck turning onto the narrow winding drive.

Jac frowned. "Hey, isn't that…"

She'd obviously reached the same conclusion I had, and it wasn't good. "You need to find a place to hide." I aimed her toward the rear of the cabin.

She spun around, lips pursed, ready to fight. "What about you? You need to come with me."

"He'll scent us the minute he gets out of the truck. We stand a better chance if we don't make it easy for him to find both of us."

"Damn it." She glanced at the approaching vehicle, then back at me. "Fine, but if you get hurt, I'll be the one going after your male parts with my claws instead of your sister."

I couldn't believe I was getting aroused by her threat. "I'll hold you to it, but later." I pressed a kiss to her forehead. "Now go."

She turned and disappeared around the corner of the building.

I'd never backed away from a fight, and I wasn't going to start now. I had a mate, a family, a future, and I wasn't about to let anyone take it away from me. I walked to the front of the cabin and waited for Shane to get out of the truck.

As a rule, shifters fought with claws and fangs. I hadn't expected him to be carrying a gun or have him aim it at my chest.

Shane sauntered toward me. "Reese, what are you

doing here?" He didn't seemed disturbed by my presence and the tone of his voice confirmed it.

"I could ask you the same thing. Though, after finding my stolen lumber, the only question I have is why." My wolf didn't care about the intricacies of the human world. Shane was a threat to our mate, one he wanted to remove. I clenched my fists, straining to keep the animal under control.

Shane shrugged, ignoring my question. "You're a lot more resourceful than I thought." He'd stopped before getting too close, no doubt factoring in the possibility of me going for the gun. He would have been right. The weapon he carried could do a lot of damage to a human, but being a shifter gave me an advantage. Add in my special military training and Shane was smart to keep his distance. Even if I lunged, I wouldn't reach him before he pulled the trigger.

"I was supposed to meet with Mick and John last night. When they didn't show up, I checked around and found out they were being held in the Hanford jail. I thought I'd have a few more days before you figured things out. I planned to have everything moved before you made your way out here."

During the time I'd worked with Shane, I learned he was boastful and loved to hear himself speak. Keeping him talking bought me more time and kept Jac safe. I tipped my head to the right. "I assume some of the equipment I found in those storage containers came from your employer's company."

"Stuff goes missing from sites all the time." He acted as if it was a bonus that came with his supervisory position. "It's a profitable side business."

"That still doesn't explain why you're stealing from me."

"Do you know how hard it is for a shifter to go to prison, to be confined and unable to let his animal truly run?"

I didn't answer, unsure what his question had to do with the current situation. The intensity of his gaze and the red darkening Shane's cheeks told me an explanation was forthcoming.

"My cousin, Dale, suffers. His wolf suffers ever day because of your family and you."

I shook my head. "I'm sorry. I have no idea what you're talking about."

"He worked for Desmond Bishop, and you—" He gritted his teeth. "You made sure he got locked up for a very long time. Stealing from you isn't even close to getting payback, but it's a start."

It didn't take long for me to make the connection and visualize the male he was talking about. Reminding Shane that his cousin was in jail because he'd kidnapped Mandy wouldn't do any good. Dale was lucky to be alive. Nick's wolf had come close to killing him. There was no reasoning with a wild wolf when it went feral, especially when it involved his mate.

Shane's angry intensified. It was an expression I'd seen before, a faraway psychotic look that told me there'd be no reasoning with him either.

His gaze snapped to the present, and he sniffed the air, then glanced past me toward the cabin. "Where's that pretty little mate of yours? I can smell her all over you. Maybe I'll show her what it's like to be fucked by a real wolf before I kill you."

A low, feral growl rumbled from my chest. My wolf snarled, gnashed his teeth, strained to be set free, to force a shift. "She's gone. I sent her for help."

"You're lying. She's close by. Her scent is strong." He frowned and glanced to his left, expecting her to appear. He inhaled again. "Actually, it's really strong."

A barely noticeable movement in the upper branches of the tree behind Shane drew my attention. I remained motionless, afraid the slightest misstep on my part would alert him to the cream-colored cat preparing to pounce.

I bit back an angry growl, wondering if there was ever going to be a time when my mate did anything she was told.

***

JAC

"You're lying. She's close by. Her scent is strong. Actually, it's really strong."

I listened to Shane and took note of his agitated state. He anxiously glanced around, searching for signs of me on the ground. I knew it was a risk to get this close, that it wouldn't be long before his wolf informed him of my true location. I didn't care, because Reese was in trouble.

Shane was the lowest form of asshole on the planet. There was no honor in pointing a gun at another shifter. We used our animals, their claws and fangs, to settle disputes when required within our community.

I regretted my decision not to let Reese tear him apart the day I met him at the construction site. If I had, maybe he wouldn't be standing on the ground below me, threatening to kill my mate.

Once I'd recognized the driver of the truck, I knew Shane had to be the person orchestrating the thefts. If he was anything like Mick and John, he wasn't going to let Reese and me live long enough to share our discovery with anyone.

I'd seen firsthand how Reese's military background enabled him to think calmly and handle danger with precision. We were newly mated, and the primal instinct to protect pulsed through both of us, even more so through him since he was a dominant male. I didn't want to hinder his logic to access and deal with the situation. My mate needed to be able to focus on the threat and not me. It was the reason I'd agreed to hide. It didn't mean I planned to stay hidden or that I wouldn't use my own skills to help him.

As soon as I disappeared behind the cabin, it was easy to get up on the roof and listen to their conversation. Shane producing a weapon changed my plans for a frontal attack. I knew enough about what happened with Desmond Bishop to know the males he'd employed were dangerous.

Shane was motivated by revenge, which made him unpredictable and deadly. Since my cat was smaller, I had a better chance if I attacked in my animal form. Because she was a hybrid with underlying traces of jaguar, most shifters were confused by her scent. They also expected her to be bigger, something I could use to my benefit.

After shedding my clothes and shifting, I'd used the treetops to circle behind him. I would only get one chance to surprise Shane. I needed to be patient, to wait for him to be distracted and hopefully lower his aim away from Reese's chest. Though Reese pretended not to see me, the angry glint in his eyes and the stiffness in his shoulders told me he was furious that I planned to interfere. I'd gladly risk my life and accept his anger if it meant he would live.

"Jac, I know you're in the tree above me. Show yourself, or I'll shoot your mate." Shane kept his weapon aimed at Reese as he took several steps backward, then lined up his back with the tree's trunk.

So much for a surprise attack. From this angle, there was no way I'd be able to jump and disarm him. I moved farther out on the branch so Shane could see me, hoping my compliance would buy Reese and me more time.

"What the hell are you?"

I knew my cat's appearance was unusual, but I'd never seen anyone's eyes get that wide. Even my father's disdain didn't compare to Shane's disgust-filled grimace. I snarled and hissed, my animal and I enraged by his insulting reaction.

I scented Shane's fear right before he raised the weapon and pulled the trigger. The bullet missed me by inches. It clipped the side of the branch, sending chunks of bark flying.

"No!" Reese yelled, already racing toward Shane.

Before Shane could fire again, a brown wolf rushed from the trees on Shane's right. He sprang into the air and sank his teeth into Shane's forearm. The momentum took both of them to the ground, knocking the gun from his hand. As soon as Shane rolled onto his stomach and crawled toward his weapon, the wolf was on him again. This time the animal sank his teeth into Shane's shoulder, pinning him so he couldn't shift.

Shane screamed, bucked, and grabbed whatever fur he could reach with his free arm, trying to dislodge the growling wolf.

A second wolf, huge, with silky black fur, which I assumed was Nick, skidded to a stop next to Reese. He snarled, pacing back and forth, ready to tear into Shane if the brown wolf needed assistance.

"Dad, stop! We need him alive," Reese said.

The brown wolf locked gazes with Reese, his growls reduced to a rumble. He gave Shane's arm one last hard shake, then reluctantly released him. Blood covered his muzzle, but not in the quantity smeared around the bite mark on Shane's skin. Nick's wolf took an imposing step forward, a warning to let Shane know he didn't have a problem finishing the job Clayton had started.

Reese retrieved the gun, removed the magazine, then tucked the weapon in the waistband along the back of his jeans. He tipped his head back and glanced in my direction. "Are you okay?" His deep voice crackled with concern.

I replied with my cat's version of an affirmative answer. Now that the situation was under control and I was no longer at risk of being shot at again, I jumped from the tree.

Nick had shifted into his human form and was standing next to me, naked. "Reese, your mate is all kinds of cute."

I growled when he stretched out his hand as if he was going to pet me.

"Jac, stop glaring at Nick." Reese snatched me off the ground and rubbed his hand along my fur. "I'd rather not have to explain to Mandy why you neutered my brother for teasing me about your cat."

Nick covered his groin and quickly backed away from us. "Damn, Jac. It was a compliment. I swear."

**

REESE

"What part of 'hide' didn't you understand?" I had Jac wrapped tightly in my arms the minute she'd landed on the ground after returning to the roof to shift into her human form and get dressed. Tension coursed through every nerve in my body. The calm I desperately needed after witnessing her near miss with Shane's bullet continued to elude me.

My father had saved Jac's life, and for that, I would forever be grateful. It didn't, however, mean I wanted my mate to see the male members of my family naked. Upon my nonnegotiable insistence, Nick and my father had gone inside and retrieved the blankets Jac and I had used the previous night, then wrapped them around their waists.

While I'd waited for Jac, and after receiving congratulations from Nick and my father on our mating, they explained how they'd found us. After Bart gave them the same information he'd given me, my father and brother decided they could get here faster if they shifted.

The rest of my family had taken the road and, depending on the conditions, were due to arrive soon. In the meantime, the males had been wise enough to stay out of my way and give me the space I needed to be with my mate. They were currently watching over Shane to make sure he didn't try to leave.

"What part of 'I have a problem with authority' didn't you understand? Being a mate means being a full partner. It means we take care of each other. The responsibility can't be one-sided." She slid her hands across my shoulders, then pulled herself up until she had her legs wrapped around my waist. "You're my mate. I love you and will always have your back, so deal with it."

I braced my arms under her ass. "You love me." It was amazing the soothing effect those three words had on my system.

She frowned and wrinkled her nose. "Did you hear anything else I said?"

"Yes." I grinned. "You said you loved me."

"Totally hopeless." Jac sighed and dropped her head on my shoulder.

"There they are." My father sounded relieved as he glanced at the truck pulling into the narrow drive.

Preston barely had the vehicle stopped before Berkley and Mandy had their doors open and were rushing toward us.

I lowered Jac to the ground seconds before Berkley had me around the neck in one of her vise-grip hugs.

"You're okay." She released me, then did the same thing to Jac.

"Fine, but you missed all the fun." Jac gave me a teasing wink.

I glared back, promising retribution later.

Berkley's gaze bounced from the partially covered bite mark on Jac's shoulder back to me. "You're mated." She smirked at Mandy, who was taking Nick's blanket in exchange for the bundle of clothes she had in her arms. "I told you so."

She had me by the neck again. "Congratulations! I'm so happy for you guys."

"Thanks." I returned the hug, glad my sister shared my

joy, but anxious to get back to the lodge so I could spend some time alone with Jac.

"So you were right." Nick zipped his pants as he strolled toward us barefoot. "Does that mean you're going to do that girly thing where you get all emotional and cry?" he chided and nudged Berkley's shoulder.

"I'll show you girly." She caught the back of his leg with her foot and shoved him at the same time. Nick flailed his arms, but it didn't stop him from falling backward and landing ass first in a puddle of muddy water.

Mandy covered her mouth to keep from laughing, then shook her head and held the blanket she was holding out to Nick. "Now that you're covered in mud, I guess you'll be riding in the back of the truck—*alone*."

"What happened to mate loyalty?" Nick pretended to reach for the blanket, then grabbed her wrist.

Mandy squealed when she landed on top of him with her hands and knees in the puddle. "Nick, I swear…" She giggled, then gave him a kiss and smeared his cheeks with mud in the process.

Preston, who'd been standing quietly next to Jac watching my sibling's antics, patted her on the shoulder. "Welcome to the family. I have a feeling you're going to fit right in." He walked over to Shane's truck and lowered the tailgate. "Maybe we should think about heading back."

"I couldn't agree more." My father had finished getting dressed and was dragging Shane toward our group.

Though his wounds had started to heal, Shane continued to clutch his arm. He also hadn't uttered a word, not since Nick threatened to rip him apart.

"Come on," my father said as he hoisted Shane onto the vehicle's bed, then jumped in next to him. "The police in Hanford are expecting you."

"I guess I'm not riding alone anymore." Nick tossed Mandy, who was as muddy as he was, over his shoulder and headed for the back of Preston's vehicle.

"I'll wait for you guys in the truck," Berkley said, then

followed after Nick and Mandy.

I pulled Jac into my arms and nuzzled her neck. "I did hear what you said about being partners and taking care of each other."

"You did?" She tipped her head back and giggled when I scooped her off the ground and headed for the truck.

"Yes, and I have a few ideas of how you can take care of me once we get home." I loved my mate and couldn't imagine my life without her. It wasn't going to be easy, but I would work on letting her help me, instead of always being the one who took care of everyone else.

ABOUT THE AUTHOR

Rayna Tyler is an author of paranormal and sci-fi romance. She loves writing about strong sexy heroes and the sassy heroines who turn their lives upside down. Whether it's in outer space or in a supernatural world here on Earth, there's always a story filled with adventure.

Printed in Great Britain
by Amazon